Praise for the Base Branch Series

"Megan Mitcham's books are well-paced, well-plotted suspense novels edged with stunning sensual intensity. Her lovers are cold and deadly--except when they are skin-to-skin. I can't wait for the next book in the series!"

- **DELILAH DEVLIN**
New York Times and USA Today bestselling author

"Nail-biter all the way to the end."

- **Michelle**, MsRomanticReads
Adult Romance & Erotic Book Reviews

"This is a fresh and exciting story with lots of great characters."

- **5 Star Amazon Review**, Enemy Mine

"Megan now joins my elite team of must read authors. I fell in love with her work in *Enemy Mine*, and it just gets better the more I read."

- **TNT Reviews**

BOOKS BY MEGAN MITCHAM

BASE BRANCH NOVELS
ENEMY MINE
JUSTICE MINE
STRANGER MINE
WARRIOR MINE
DANGER MINE - July 2015
PRISONER MINE - January 2016
SURVIVOR MINE - April 2016

BUREAU NOVELS
FOR ALL TO SEE
PAINTED WALLS - October 2015

BLACKLIST SERIES
VERSIONS
VIRTUES - 2016

BOX SET
HEARTS IN DANGER - June 2015
benefiting The American Heart Association

ANTHOLOGIES
ANTICIPATION
CONQUESTS - 2015
ROGUE HEARTS - 2015
SEX OBJECTS - 2016
COWBOY HEAT
HIGH OCTANE HEROES
WILD AT HEART VOLUME II
benefiting Turpentine Creek Wildlife Refuge

Stranger Mine

Base Branch Novel #3

Megan Mitcham

Published By MM Publishing LLC
Edited by Lacey Thacker
Cover Design by Deranged Doctor Design

Stranger Mine
All Rights Are Reserved. Copyright 2014 by Megan Mitcham
First electronic publication: October 2014
First print publication: October 2014

Digital ISBN: 978-1-941899-04-5

Print ISBN: 978-1-941899-05-2

To my Diamond Dolls for welcoming, teaching, encouraging, and loving me and all things romance.

Chapter One

A rock-hard boner sure as shit made running difficult. Ryan hustled from the center-console Wellcraft, his boots creating thunder across the sun-bleached wood. He bounded from the dock over a three-foot sea wall. The tarmac sucked at his soles. He pushed harder across the private airfield to a waiting bird. The loaded plate carrier, battle belt, ruck, M4, and assorted weaponry strapped to every part of his body hugged him like an old friend. Its weight and the adrenaline triple shot of mission readiness provided the minuscule provocation his sex soldier needed to stand at attention and salute.

Curse Sloan Harris—McCord, now—to England and back. Why had he listened to her advice in the first place? "Kick your mommy's hand-picked harem of socialites, along with her ass, to the curb, and find your own center," his best friend said. Didn't mean he had to comply with either directive. But screw it all, or none in his case, he'd heard the truth in her words.

The only thing he'd found the center of in the last year and a half was his palm. And ole righty didn't do much to take the edge off his razor-sharp libido. Gritty wind hurled from the *whooshing* blades. It slapped his face and he squinted, seeing the open door of the copter through a thin slit and forest of lashes. The engine's rumble filled his ears. He leaped into the gray belly of the Blackhawk and sat in the middle seat facing the cockpit. Though really, his rock-hard wood made the whole thing a cockpit. He shoved on the helmet from the seat to his left and livened the comm so he could communicate with the flight crew.

A deep voice crackled to life through the communication link. "Welcome aboard, sir. Call sign, please."

"Sierra. Hotel. Echo. Papa. Hotel. Echo. Romeo. Delta. One. Nine. Nine. Six." Ryan ticked the words off like they were tattooed on his tongue.

"Good deal," the pilot said, "now Sammy here doesn't have to shoot you."

"That'd have put a real cramp in my day," Ryan acknowledged.

"Mine too," a soft and painfully feminine voice whispered in his ear. *Sammy, no doubt, now, was short for Samantha.* Through the gap between the seat and padded metal wall, Ryan spied the pilot's small hand holstering an M1911. Her honeyed voice and pistol-pride for his own Brownings caused the blood to pulse in his dick. "I'd have been cleaning bits of you out of my baby for days," she added with a pat to the aircraft's panel. The throb ebbed, but not the swelling.

He laughed and focused too much attention on not strangling his vital organ with the harness and buckle. "Ready when you are."

"Whirlybird ready," the co-pilot said.

"Sit back, relax, and we'll have you to the drop at 2100. Hope you like to feel the sea spray, 'cause we're flying low," Sammy purred.

Relax? Right. If anyone looked at his trip itinerary—Cabo San Lucas, beachfront villa, and saltwater fishing boat rentals—they'd assume he'd come for pleasure. The hum of the rotors shifted and steady vibrations jiggled his ass as the Hawk lifted off the tarmac. Dust danced in whipping funnels around them. Despite his fake itinerary and ragging hard-on, this trip was all business.

Ryan shifted his hips in an effort to alleviate the ache in his groin. When Sloan's words slammed him in the gut, he should have moved out of his parent's city condo and gotten a place of his own. But no. Instead he swore off the women his mother insisted on setting him up with on a bi-weekly basis.

Dumb as dirt, Noble.

He'd cowed to his mother's wishes since his life altering, unhappy tenth birthday. What person wouldn't when they saw their world's anchor, the strongest person they'd ever known, break before their eyes? Especially if he were the cause of the pain.

Any mention of his moving out and the woman shed tears like the conduit for all water sources on the planet. While they zipped over the great blue Pacific, Ryan's gut twisted in perfect sailor's knots just thinking about the impending conversation. He stretched his legs out and focused on the positive. His cock had shriveled like the coward he was.

The usual lightness that accompanied Ryan while in the air never came. Not even buzzing the rod holders of the rented boat stirred him. The sky was blotted in shades of red and orange by the setting sun, but it could have been black for all he cared. At some point he'd have to rip away the security blanket he provided his mother. And really, when he wasn't lying to himself—something he'd become very adept at—he admitted his fear of losing the protection she provided him. The fake life he'd lead, like the fake itinerary, looked good from the outside and hid his inadequacies well.

The gray face, black numbers and hands on Ryan's watch read 1930. Time to get out of his head and into the mission. He pulled the topographical map and satellite pictures from the pocket on his left thigh and smoothed them over his lap. With the sun snuggling the horizon, Ryan deciphered the rings, grid, and numbers by the green glow of the instruments.

"Fucking desert," he mumbled.

"At least it's not summer, man," the co-pilot chimed. "You'd bake to death within an hour of Sonoran heat exposure."

Sammy guffawed. "Yeah. You'll be as uncomfortable as shit in the near freezing temperatures, especially if it rains, but you won't die. Not from the elements. Huh, Mike?"

"Hell no," Mike cried. "You screw with El Chapo, he'll make soup out of your hide and you'll die listening to the sound of your own screams."

"Well, that's comforting," Ryan quipped.

"I'm serious, man. You're crazy to do anything in Mexico. These cartels don't fuck around. You screw with their operation, shit, you even think about it, you get dead. And Sinaloa is one of the worst." The pilot rattled on, fear quavering his voice as he recounted the horror stories he'd heard from his years flying over the embattled country.

America's greed for the forbidden and an armload of Mexican men's hunger for power and prosperity, both unconcerned about the cost of their addictions, fueled the drug and sex-slave trade that funneled from the southern border into the States. The gruesome images playing in Ryan's head weren't some battlefield hearsay, but knowledge gained from the ground over the last year of bone-grinding work. All of which was set to culminate this February night with simultaneous hits across the cartel leader's key compounds.

By sunrise the next day the Mexican government would miraculously have "El Chapo" Guzmán Loera in custody. And several of his drug and human-trafficking facilities would be burned to cinder. If everything went according to plan.

Chapter Two

Heat radiated up the collar of Ryan's desert-brush BDU's, chasing away the chill of the night air. Since Commander Tucker had planned the mission, the moon hid behind a thick layer of clouds. The veil obscured his and the other teams' trek in cavernous dark. With no artificial lights for twenty miles or more to the northwest in Caborca and the same southeast in Hermosillo, Ryan saw the landscape in shades of gray through the single lens of the thermal imagery monocular strapped to his head.

Low bracken scraped his pant legs and threatened to entangle his boots for the twelve miles. He maintained a brisk jog, shoving the sting in his lungs and calves to the back of his mind. Sandy soil finally gave way to the crunch of rocks under his thick soles and he slowed his pace to about six miles an hour. Only three miles left until he reached the crop of three buildings. The most treacherous three miles, as he'd nearly discovered the hard way.

The cartel liked their early warning systems oh so well. Ryan scowled at the first of thousands of anti-personnel land mines buffering the Sinaloa compound. On his first reconnaissance mission eight months ago, he'd stumbled upon the cylindrical death trap. He'd swear the thing had winked at him. His only saving grace had been its layer's lazy dig job. The guy probably figured he was at the end of the boundary and if this one didn't get the enemy, then one of the two-thousand-plus others would do the trick. In his previous three ventures, Ryan had mapped each of the bastards in the three-mile long, three-foot wide strip he now ran. He prayed he hadn't missed any.

The covert sector of the United Nations, known as The Base Branch, existed on a plane so covert the Vice President of the United States of America didn't even know it operated right under his nose. The agency employed the elite from across the globe and operated bases in Europe and the US. Their singular goal was maintaining and fostering peace. In order to keep peace, oftentimes they had to do the shit no one wanted to do, like crawl through the dirt scoping out explosives in the freezing desert temps.

Ryan and his cohorts maintained the quavering scale of peace with sharp efficiency. Even they, the elite's elite, hadn't expected booby traps and guards three miles away from the compound. Nothing if not quick studies, they discovered that when it came to protecting their investments, the Sinaloa cartel risked nada. They took precautions like a man with the only daughter on a pirate ship would—and then some.

Ryan dropped to his knees a mile away from his destination and steadied his breath. Two minutes passed. Then one more. The patrol was late. He didn't have time for tardiness. Every team planned to radio mission-ready five minutes before go time. If even one didn't call in, the mission and all their blood, sweat, and tears—well, he didn't cry, but someone probably did—would be for naught.

When the rattle of the Jeep engine pierced the night, his decision to press on without taking out the first tier guards skidded to a halt. He ducked behind a small boulder in the middle of nowhere. With the foothills still another two miles away, it seemed the small mountain range ostracized the offending hunk of earth, chunking it from its brethren. Thank goodness. The headlights swung across the rock as it turned, following the horseshoe-shaped dirt road that didn't host a mass of land mines.

Like every other time, the dusty vehicle stopped ten feet past the boulder. Only this time the driver didn't exit. Neither did the two passengers. Ryan's hair stood on end. He sheathed the KABAR he'd planned on using, flipped on his Base comm, and grabbed the M4 slung across his chest. The radio didn't crackle. As it should, the line maintained silence. When bullet spray didn't alight the world around him, he eased centimeter by precious centimeter until his monocular illuminated the open-top automobile.

Three occupants he'd previously dubbed with fitting nicknames tussled about the car. Big 'Un sat behind the wheel, body twisted and lurching as he bore his snarl onto Gnarly's crater-marked face in the passenger seat. Big 'Un shoved Bitchy so hard in the back seat only the spare tire kept his body from toppling out. The engine muffled their curses, but couldn't mute their gestures. Gnarly and Bitchy were pissed at Big 'Un about something. Their heads bobbed and index fingers shook like only a Latin mother's could, or so he'd thought.

Sweat sheened Ryan's brow, but his breath came in steady, even intervals. He dropped the riffle back to his chest and retrieved his gunmetal blade from the small of his back. Big 'Un busted his wide shoulders from the extra-medium opening, grabbed his assault riffle, waving it over his head, and continued bitching as he walked to the far end of the patrolled U.

Gnarly cut the engine and slammed his door, huffing off in the opposite direction of the first while ranting in his native tongue. "If he slips his dick inside her, the fucker is going to get it chopped off and the rest of us killed."

"Screw you too. You make me ride in back like a child then leave me stuck here," Bitchy bitched.

"Because you whine like a kid still pulling on his momma's titty." Gnarly's words drifted off as his distance increased.

"You talk about my mother and I'll kill you myself, Tomas." Bitchy climbed over the rear metal door. The gravel crunched under his shoes, growing louder by the second. They stopped a few feet from the rock. "Stupid assholes. All of you. He knows we're not supposed to touch the *Bronce*, only screw with her head. I don't know what makes her special to Gabrone."

Ryan crouched deeper and held his breath. Special to Émile Gabrone? The man known as Gabriel—because he kills those who cross him with the vengeance of the archangel—had no one in the world special to him. He killed his parents at the age of eighteen. Enslaved his sister in the sex trade by nineteen. By twenty, his rep preceded him wherever he went and earned him a place among El Chapo's highest ranks.

So, who the hell was the Bronce, the Bronze, and why was she special to Gabrone? Ryan wanted to know more than Bitchy, but didn't have time to find out.

Metal clinked on rock. The metal-on-metal whine of a zipper followed along with the unmistakable pittle pattern of free-flowing urine. The stench of ammonia confirmed it. With one fluid move, Ryan bolted around the rock. Bitchy's pitiful face didn't wrinkle in alarm until he was inches away and closing fast. He clamped the man's forehead between his bicep and forearm, then wrenched it back, locking the lean man against his chest. He struck hard and fast. The blade entered the man's neck just below his ear.

Death came quickly. Easily. Much more easily than the limp man in his arms had made it for others. More easily than he deserved. Ryan didn't enjoy killing, but he liked ridding the world of monstrous people.

"What the fuck?" The whites of Gnarly's eyes swelled as big as a boiled egg. His gun hung at his side as he struggled to comprehend what he saw in the murky dark.

Ryan didn't hesitate. He released the corpse and knife from his grip. Every muscle in his body coiled and released as he sprang. He cleared two yards on adrenaline, conditioning, and training. While he was in the air, the man reached, reeling his gun from the long strap where it dangled. The knuckles of Ryan's right fist connected with the man's jaw before the muzzle of the riffle made it to half-mast. Dust puffed around Gnarly's chambray shirt and khaki cargos as he hit the ground. Despite his size, the man's neck snapped under Ryan's well-placed hands after a firm twist.

He didn't allow himself to dwell on the sickening crack of bone, or the rippling aftershocks it sent through the man's skull, or the way it tingled his fingertips. He shucked his knife from

Bitchy, cleaned it, and stole quietly along the clear path toward Big 'Un.

The beefy man's pants hung around his ankles, but a bladder flush was the last thing on the guy's mind. His rocking hips and rhythmically pumping forearm gave him away before his words did. "Puta chula mi verga. Rápido. Más fuerza. La mujer de bronce."

It'd be nice to let him finish. But Ryan wasn't in a particularly kind mood. The constant stream of dirty talk muted the minute sounds of his approach. He'd have forgone the assistance in stealth because the display flipped his gut. It paid to be aware of your surroundings and keep *me-time* private. The big man gave the least fight.

Three bodies down. Four more to go. Then *boom*. He'd break this link in the Sinaloa's trafficking trade.

Crouched and hidden by night, Ryan sprinted like the devil dogged his heels. In the span of fourteen and a half football fields he reached the first building in the compound. He leaned against the metal exterior used for storing what the cartel called "cargo." They were mostly women and girls at this location, but others ran the gamut in slave labor. Ryan tossed the monocular into an exterior pouch on his ruck and wiped the sweat from his brow. Silently, he dragged in deep, steady breaths. From the illumination of the rear porch light of the main building, Ryan checked the time. One minute until check-in, a.k.a. midnight. Talk about cutting it close.

He had exactly thirty minutes to exterminate the rest of the staff, set a rucksack full of explosives, and blow the joint. Before shoving him out the door, the pilot had told him, "Extraction at 0230. You're not here, we blow you a peace sign to the winds and we're outta here." That gave him just enough time to haul ass over a live minefield and swan dive into the Hawk.

"Fantastic," he whispered.

He understood the tight schedule. When running a simultaneous op, you had to run tandem time or run the risk of forewarning your targets. In Ryan's case, if he stayed too long the full security force could fall on his head and do more than muss his already wild mop. This facility ran on a skeleton staff since the next shipment wasn't due for two weeks. Plenty of time to cancel the round up when they discovered they didn't have anyplace to put them. Ryan wiped the smile off his face and checked the time again. Midnight on the dot.

But not even static crackled the comm-link.

Ryan's gaze scanned the area. Not a person in sight. The main house flashed like a pre-cut diamond among dirt. A fancy pad that didn't belong in the middle of the desert. Truth be told, it didn't belong anywhere. Too much everything. From the multi-level cascading arch, terracotta roof, and the six-bay garage to the perfectly manicured flowerbeds surrounding the mansion, it screamed Beverly Hills—not Sonoran Desert hills.

Ten seconds past midnight and still not a word. Apprehension niggled. He studied the circular drive of brick pavers at the back of the house, meeting the garage at the side, and snugging up to the makeshift jailhouse. From earlier visits he knew the front of the house also boasted a paved circular drive. It all made a fancy highway system with gravel walkways and bits of bright green grass between.

"Team Alpha go." Khani's voice sounded over the airwaves. Ryan released the breath he'd held on lock-down.

Khani Slaughter, his sometimes partner, sometimes head honcho, transferred from the UK division six months ago. She'd said the move was to stay close to her brother, Zeke, who'd taken a spec-ops job stateside, and to get back in the field. The move had given Commander Tucker some dependable back-up while he was away on business and gave him the option of vacation. Not that he'd have shit to do without the job. However, rumor had it she moved to avoid someone very specific.

Right now, the tall beauty was set to attack the biggest drug trafficking organization in Mexico's history, the Sinaloa Federation, with a handful of elite warriors and an army behind them.

After the other four teams gave the go-ahead, Ryan gave his. "Zeta go." And he went. Hard and fast.

Chapter Three

Piper had always hated running. Amazing how circumstances changed a person's point of view. She'd give Émile Gabrone's left nut to run ten miles without slowing. Shoot, she'd give that for nothing at all. But Lord, she wanted to run full out. To inhale fresh air. To feel the dry heat slap her in the face. A smile spread across her sweat-slicked mug. One more interrogation and she'd have everything she needed. Then she could do away with the bastard. The only decision left was how she wanted to end his atrocious life.

The chain *clanged* in time with her hops. Maybe she'd choke him to death with her jump rope. Jump chain, really. The makeshift exercise tool worked to a point. Double-unders were out of the question. She'd already beamed herself on the forehead too many times to count. A whack on the shin hurt ten times worse. As a result, her timing and jumping skills had grown ten-fold in the last two months.

Damn good thing she didn't have big boobs. She'd have been hard pressed to craft a makeshift bra. The scrap of fabric holding the end of her ponytail and the pile of shirts she'd stuffed into another for a pillow stretched the limits of her crafting abilities.

When her count reached five hundred, Piper leaped out of the arch like she played Double Dutch with her sisters, Sparrow and Ivy. Only in this game, she turned one-hundred-eighty degrees, grabbed the links with both hands, and tugged, shifting all her weight to her left leg. The metal cuff bit into her right wrist. Blood seeped from the scabs ringing her upper hand, but the crimson didn't pour like it had when they were fresh. Ten feet of quarter-inch torus links swirled and danced in the air. The dull metal finally shuddered to a uniform line from her hands to the U-bolt protruding from the cinderblock wall.

She walked toward the wall, allowing the chain to bow low then pool. Pitching forward, she let gravity take her face first to the gritty slab and caught herself, palms flat, in the plank position. If she ever made it back home, she could always open a gym. She could cater to a specific niche—people with ten feet or less of workout space. She needed a job. And she mastered the ten-foot workouts six weeks ago. *Welcome to Master Vega's ten-foot gym.* The mortgage on the place would be bearable, even for California real estate.

Her arms burned at one hundred. By two hundred they seared. But what the hell else did she have to do until Gabrone returned? Not a damn thing. At three hundred and fifty-four, she froze and kicked an ear toward the thick metal door across the room.

Pop. Pop. Pop.

She shouldn't be able to hear in the soundproofed room. Yet, her senses had honed over time. When she was the lone occupant and when she wasn't singing at the top of her lungs or rattling chains like an old haunt, she could hear the gravel outside the door crunch under approaching boots, and more times than she liked to remember, she'd heard gun shots.

The number of shots usually coincided with the number of men who tried to feel her up or fuck her. If they were stupid enough to get close, she made sure they left the guesthouse—as she liked to call it—with a broken bone. A nose. An arm. A finger. She'd have loved to bite the cock off of the big son of a bitch that threatened to shove it between her lips earlier, but his compadres had convinced him to stick to the job. *Damn it.*

Maybe Gabrone came back early and caught wind of it? If she went by the shots, three of them got tapped between the eyes. For some extremely incomprehensible reason, Émile Gabrone had claimed her as his own without actually claiming her body. Which wasn't something she'd looked forward to by any means, but it was something she'd mentally prepared for...as much as a person could. Aside from the chain and seclusion, the man treated her like a queen. He wanted her to love him. He wanted them to grow old together. So, he wooed her. Captive style. Every night he arranged for a bath and fresh clothes to be brought in for her and privacy for the task. Every day brought three meals. Nothing fancy, but she wouldn't complain. She didn't have to cook the food or clean up after. Except for the whole no-coming-and-going thing, she had it made.

Chapter Four

Ryan didn't even like surprise birthday parties. He sure as shit didn't like surprise goons. Five extra men stood between him and mission success. Double the number he and the planning team had expected. Sweat rolled down his face, trickled the length of his torso, and tickled his inner thigh. Killing was hard work, especially when the targets were trained killers themselves.

Holstering his sidearm, Ryan grimaced at the three bodies littering the hallway, then stepped back into the office. He slipped the knife from the body slumped across the paper-strewn desk and truly hoped the clerk was the last of them. His forearm quivered with exhaustion and his stomach gave a sympathetic shudder.

I kill so the good may live. That the light may equal the dark. That the world maintains her balance.

Breath blew through his lips in a calming pull and push of his lungs as he recited part of the creed, the foundation, of the Base Branch.

While he reminded himself he wasn't a bloodthirsty monster, he kept an ear on the doorway. His eyes scanned the computer screen. "Mother fucker." His entire body clenched in pure rage, obliterating his bid for serenity. The force of his blow gouged the tip of his blade into the cherry wood. "Why the hell else would they need five extra guys, Noble?" He raged at himself, since the rest of them were dead.

When most people thought about gangs and cartels, they imagined haphazard chaos. In reality, they kept better records than the IRS. They knew where every cent came from and where it went. Sure they lost shipments and payments in transit and at the border, but they knew exactly how much, who stopped their money from getting back to them, and where they lived.

Ryan read the flat screen monitor once more to make certain he hadn't lost his mind. Too bad he hadn't. The open spreadsheet had several columns, but two interested him most. Type and date. The type jumped back and forth between goods, which meant drugs, or cargo, which meant people. They had a shipment of cargo due to arrive in two days, not two weeks like their source had said. This meant the cargo had already been gathered, whether by coercion or force, and were en route.

The hands on his watch flipped him the bird, telling him he had fifteen minutes to set the charges and leave. Not even enough time for all the C-4 in his ruck, but still enough time to exert maximum damage to the facility. His conscience wagged its finger. For the truckload of women it wouldn't matter that the Sinaloa lost their leader and several key buildings in their network. Time and disorganization would eventually eat at the cartel, but for a while things would run as though nothing had changed. The cogs El Chapo placed long ago would continue turning until they caught up with the news, realized their leaders dropped like the stock market, and that their guaranteed payments were no longer a sure thing.

Doomed from the outset. Ryan tried to convince himself that the women on the truck were doomed regardless of his actions, but he didn't believe himself. Ever the loyal soldier, he shoved the unease aside, stowed his knife, and slung the ruck onto the table. He had a mission to complete and a HELO to catch.

He set six charges in the main house, which boasted a kitchen fit for Easton Wells. During the short time he'd visited his old partner, Sloan, in London, the butler she'd married into had whipped up the meanest meals of his entire life in a kitchen this size. Too bad none of these thugs put this kitchen to proper use. They had no problem utilizing the eight bedrooms and nearly as many bathrooms. The fuckers had all the amenities you could ask for, and in the middle of the desert no less. Even a pool table and a flat screen big enough to make him weep.

In the detached garage, he skimped, only setting one on a blacked-out Suburban and one high on the back wall.

Time check. Six minutes.

Ryan bolted, churning the gravel and kicking up dust as he cleared the forty yards between the garage and prison. A spotlight from the main house centered the only entrance and exit on the twenty-by-thirty shed. Had it housed tools or lawn equipment, the building itself wouldn't have held menace, but knowing thirty or more people per delivery had been crammed into the meager confines at near constant intervals over the last five years made the tan metal structure a house of horrors.

He could place four charges on the exterior walls and call it good. Even with no one inside, the thought of seeing the inside of the clandestine jail chilled the heated skin of his nape. Guilt would eat at him whether he went inside or not. Why haunt himself further with images that would be so similar to the alternate lockup where they'd send the next shipment?

Two balls of explosive clay warmed in his hands. When he stopped, the structure loomed overhead like a monster. Ryan extended his hand toward the corner and placed one ball on the exterior where one point of structural load met the corner post. He slipped a charge from the ruck draped over his chest and pressed the metal end into the pliable material.

"You fucking coward." His own voice sounded harsh to his ears.

Why could he kill people? Stare a bullet, blade, or bully in the eyes and never blink, but not speak his fucking mind? If he wasn't going to radio the commander and tell him to hell with his plan, if he wasn't going to tell his mother he'd had enough of her running his life, then by God, the least he could do was face down the interior of a building and rig it to blow into a million tiny pieces correctly.

Ryan's hand slid over the L-shaped handle and yanked the lever toward the ground. The blasted thing only budged an eighth of an inch. Locked. He didn't have shit for time to find a key, and he didn't feel like getting shot by ricochet. His size fourteens glistened as he raised his knee to his chest. Ignoring the blood, Ryan slammed his heel into the metal. Once. Twice. The third blow sent the handle skittering over the rocks. With a flip of the locking mechanism, he opened the door and hung in suspended animation for several heartbeats.

Of all the times for his cock to rear its head, staring into the wary brown eyes of a woman chained to a wall was the worst possible time—even

if the sight of her made his heart race as though
he'd just completed a HALO leap out of the cargo
hole without his chute. Thank the extraction gods
he'd been trained in high stress, and even higher
danger, situations for the last seven years. Finally
the experience kicked his ass into gear.

"My name is Ryan Noble. I won't hurt you."
He spoke in Spanish, using as gentle a voice as he
could muster while the lower half of his body
attempted mutiny. "I'm going to place some
explosives. Then I'll release you."

Her back remained rigid against the gray
cinderblock wall. Leanly muscled arms peeked out
from a white tank. As though they had also bound
her legs to her narrow chest, her knees nearly
grazing the bottom of her chin. Fear may have
hidden someplace deep inside her sweaty exterior,
but curiosity and suspicion ran the schooled set of
her square jaw and alert eyes. Her gaze followed his
boot treads through the door and to the far wall
opposite the cleat securing the length of chain to
the wall.

"Where is your home? How long have you
been here? How were you captured? What's your
name? Are you injured?" In an attempt to alleviate
the guarded furrow of her brow and gain some
information, he talked while he worked his way
toward her, placing charges as he went. Yet, each
inquiry collided with stony silence.

On the wall nearest his surprise guest, Ryan
averted his gaze to the creamy clay in his hand. He
observed her through his periphery and posed the
same questions again in English, and then
Portuguese. Irritation worked his jaw as he tossed
the remaining explosives into his pack, zipped it,
and slung it onto his back. Ten feet away from the

captive, he crouched to give her space and protect himself.

One last time he asked his questions, using sign language. It was worth a try. The set of her almond eyes and the slope of her pert, rounded-tip nose spoke to no other possible heritage. Dark brown hair, nearly black from the wetness, snugged to her head in a plaited braid obscured by her position. The natural tan of her complexion said Latin American. Luscious lips that didn't fit the sharp box of her regal jaw pursed in the first hint of reaction since he'd laid eyes on her.

But again she didn't speak. Ryan glanced at the gray face of his watch. No more time to waste. He stood. "I'm going to release you. Can you run?" Again, no response. Warily, he stepped over a defined ring of dirt piled in a semi-circle around her, like she'd claimed her territory and used the tiny mound as a Do Not Enter sign.

On his spin around the sparse room he hadn't seen any place to hide a key, and like the lock on the door, he didn't have time to search for one. He'd have preferred to use his boot on the U-bolt, but the thing hitched at chest level to the gray brick. He wasn't that flexible. Ryan pulled his assault riffle from his neck and used the butt as a hammer, ramming the curved metal in a series of vicious down strokes. The bolt proved more difficult than the door handle, bending yet refusing to break. He slung the gun over his shoulder and grabbed the chain with both hands.

Rounded links grew teeth and gnawed his palms as he heaved heavenward. For once, pumping stacked bars of weights instead of beautiful woman seemed worth the ungratifying effort. The U bent like slow-moving taffy, defying gravity. When he released his grip, red stained the creases of his left hand. He wiped his palm over the only clean spot he found on his fatigues, switched his grip, and tugged the crooked U toward the floor. Finally one side broke away. The jagged, patterned edges scraped the link as he shimmied and jerked it off the end.

"If it's too heavy, I can help carry the chain. We have to move. Now." Ryan shoved his right arm through the strap of the M4 dangling around his neck then crouched within kissing distance of the woman's gorgeous face to gather the heap.

The brunt of her bare forehead slammed into the bridge of his nose with blinding speed and instantaneous, brain-numbing pain. He teetered on the balls of his feet and fought the urge to grab his nose. His left hand shot for the wall while his right covered his sidearm. A few hits he could take. A bullet, not so much. His experiences with them hadn't been all that great, and he'd rather not deal with one ripping his skin apart in the middle of the desert.

Ryan braced for the next blow, but it didn't come. She apparently had no damn trouble toting the weight. The tinny chain rattled its way across the room and out the door in a matter of seconds. Urging his eyelids open, his vision met with watery blurs of light. He coaxed the tears from his eyes with swipes of his fists, but new moisture gathered like Stephen Strasburg fans at the end of a Nationals game.

Screw it. He was on his feet and running before the world presented itself to his hesitant vision. Luckily he'd oriented his brain to the room enough before impact that he knew where the door stood and remembered the drop to ground level. Following the incessant rattle of chains, he reached mid-yard before his sight returned. Sharp copper tang seeped into his mouth and he spat the blood onto the stitch of grass before leaping onto the deck.

When he reached the open back door, several things struck him at once. Thankfully none of them was a bullet or a forehead. Number one, why was he chasing after a woman who attacked him when he should be high-tailing it in the opposite direction? Two, did he look dangerous? It may sound vain, but based on the reviews he'd collected over his sexual prime, he was a charismatic eye-catcher. Not someone who elicited fight-or-flight instincts. Not from women anyway. Third, if it turned out her loyalty sat with the Sinaloa, would he kill her? Fourth, if he ran like a world-class marathoner, didn't trip on a land mine and end up critter chow, would he make his damn extraction on time?

Chapter Five

"Should have prayed for wisdom, amor."

Sierra Vega's voice sing-songed in Piper's head. She dismissed the harpy drone of her mother's go-to phrase. She'd heard it enough already. Every time things didn't go her way. Or her sisters' way. But hell, why had she prayed to run? Of all things?

Here you go, genius.

She thanked her father for her long legs and churned them out of the guest cottage. Until this blew over, she needed a hiding spot. Desperate to quiet the rattle, to conceal her location, Piper spread her fingers as wide as they could stretch and hugged the mound of chain to her chest. No way in hell would she chance a bullet hole running away with that lunatic. No way would she run into the arms of the Sinaloa grunts. Only Gabrone could make this right.

When she bound onto the gravel walkway, surprise peaked her brows. The expectation of gunshots or quick arms and groping hands fell away. Jagged rocks bruised her feet, but not a soul blocked her escape. Her heart cradled in the arms of hope, Piper drove her burning legs hard toward the garage. Breath sailed in her nose and w*hooshed* out her mouth. Half way to the garage the grass skid beneath her feet and her tight jaw gaped.

At the bottom steps, a distorted figure lay prone in the shadow. *No, surely they weren't all dead.* There had to be a different explanation for the silence.

In an instant her direction changed. She shot for the main house like an arrow. The chain disagreed with her sudden turn. It spilled out between her twisted torso and elbow. Her greedy hands clambered to contain the wayward links without slowing. Wind gusted and shoved her off balance more than the fifteen pounds of awkward metal. Her arms flailed in an effort to catch her balance. The chain plummeted to the ground. With several quick steps Piper righted herself and rushed on, leaving the bond dragging behind her.

Two yards away, the lump defined into a murdered heap of man. Blood imbrued the collar of his cream short-sleeve and pooled around the muzzle of the AK still strapped to his back. *He hadn't heard the wraith coming.* Dread overcame hope, blotting out the warmth and light inside her chest.

Piper slowed enough to hedge the body and spool the chain into two long loops. She hurried up the stairs and prayed—despite her mother's words and the real possibility that they would kill her—they weren't all dead. She'd come so close. Risked so much. This couldn't be the end.

She swallowed the lump in her throat. Silence, dead silence, deafened. The quiet she'd grown accustomed to, but only in her space. Anytime they opened the cottage door their noise accosted her. TV. Music. Cursing. Hollering. Fucking. But now...nothing.

Piper heard the whisper of stirring rocks. Her heart nearly leaped out of her body and dragged her along. Away from the warrior. Away from danger.

Regardless of his reassuring words and calm manner, awareness of him had rocked her core as soon as he stepped into her cell. The efficiency with which he placed the explosives, tracked the door, and scrutinized her with his fire-blue gaze, all while rattling off multiple languages, said elite, government agency, big agenda, avoid at all costs.

Piper hoisted the chain over her shoulder and sprinted for the second floor. Her captors had grown comfortable around her. Talked too much when they brought her food and clothing. She had no idea which room housed the office, but she knew where to start the search. Bodies littered the place like leftover take-out containers in a bachelor pad or her old apartment. She gave each grizzly scene a wide berth, but couldn't skirt the rotund stiff at the top of the staircase. She gripped the railing for leverage and kicked a leg over the sprawled man's torso. As she straddled Juan Paulo's corpse, the commando's voice reverberated through her.

"Stop where you are."

The authority of his gritty tone froze and heated her at the same time. Her fingers bit into the wooden balustrades, and she stilled as much as her heaving chest would allow. She dismissed the warmth and need that screamed inside her as exhaustion and desperation for human contact. Slowly she turned. Their gazes collided. Even across the cavernous room, her fever bloomed into an all-out forest fire, scorching a line up her spread legs, arched back, and open arms.

Hours and days of solitude. The precariousness of her situation. Either or both must have snapped the last vestiges of her sanity. Fear should have been the primal emotion boomeranging through her overwrought system.

There was no reason a man in blood-splattered battle dress and with a gun pointed at her chest should elicit anything else. But there it was. Awareness and yearning hugged her close, copping a feel of her tits and grazing the insides of her thighs. His gaze didn't wander from her face. She felt his big, lean hands exploring her body all the same.

His blue gaze remained locked on her own in steely calm. Beneath sweat-thinned war paint a muscle ticked in his broad jaw. That and the third leg in his pants gave him away. No way to miss a bulge like that. Not from the moon. Surprise embarrassment crept up her neck and settled in her cheeks. In preservation of every kind, she used the muscles she'd honed over the course of her confinement and launched herself onto the landing.

Rolling out of his line of fire, Piper spooled her torso in the chain, but kept her legs free of the obstruction. She pushed off the floor with her hands and pistoned her quads down the hallway. Thunderous footfalls rumbled on the stairs. She didn't dare look back. Instead, she aimed for a small pile of bodies at mid-hall. The heap flagged a point of interest like a blinking neon light outside her mom's tattoo parlor.

She pushed the twinge of homesickness aside and jumped over the tangle of lifeless arms and legs. Her hand slid along the wall and tightened on the metal doorframe, unique from all the other wooden ones in the house. Inside, a man slumped over a thick wooden desk. Scattered blood-soaked papers and a sleeping desktop snugged around him. The sight shouldn't have loosened the kinks of unease in her belly, but a billowy exhale puffed her cheeks all the same. "Thank God."

As soon as the words whispered from her lips the cuff on her right wrist jerked taut. Bile rose like the tide in her esophagus. She snapped her head toward the door so fast her neck popped. The sickness receded. He hadn't caught her. Not yet, at least. Piper wrapped her palm around the metal links and jerked with all her might. She never planned to play tug-of-war with a dead man. She'd done a lot of unexpected things over the last six months. Grief and a sliver of hope would make a person do anything.

And that chased away the sandman most nights.

Her obscene tail wedged between a guard's muffin top and radio clip, refusing to budge. Piper slackened the chain and flipped her wrist. The metal scraped into her skin, calling fresh blood to the surface. She tried once more, widening her stance and throwing her entire body into the motion. The links broke free and she reeled in the heavy line. He rounded the corner, gun up and ready. Again he didn't take the shot.

Piper stumbled backward into the room. She shoved both hands against the door and slammed it closed. A deadbolt never looked so good. The silver lever turned, smacking the thick latch into the sturdy frame. Not three seconds later something rammed against the metal. It *gonged* in the small room, resounding like a call to battle. A sob tore from her throat. She clamped a trembling hand over the surprising emotion and scrambled for the computer.

Chapter Six

Ryan grabbed the base of the mountain by the ankles and strained against the dead weight of three men. Inch by inch he moved them from in front of the door. With the new vantage point, he repositioned and battered the metal again. Once more the force speared up his leg in defeat, jarring his flagging hard-on into submission.

One problem down. A few more to go.

No way would he get through the door by force. The thing was prison-door solid. He could shoot through the drywall, but didn't want to chance hitting the *Bronce*. In the small prison her back had been snug to the wall. Her hair was braided close to her scalp and dripped with sweat, making it appear dark as night. But the instant he caught sight of her sprinting up the stairs he knew she was Big 'Un's bronze fantasy. The copper of her long plait grazed the lean lines of her back, ending at the natural curve of her waist.

Shamed though he was, he had his own quick and dirty fantasies about the Bronce. They'd come in on swift, razor-sharp wings, stealing his breath. He'd given her reason to run this time. But Lord, he couldn't tamp down his reaction to her soulful eyes, strength, and body made for endurance sex. Ryan never enjoyed killing, but he might have enjoyed killing these men, if he'd first found her locked up like no animal should be.

Time for finesse. He pulled two thin, metal strips from the pouch on his PIG vest. The tension tool slid easily into the key slot's base. The rake scraped over the tumbler pins as his hands worked. After two attempts, Ryan turned the lock ever so slowly. He nested the tool back into its case, drew the H&K, then immediately holstered the damn thing.

The perfect opportunity to end this had presented itself on the staircase and he didn't take the shot. Bench him forever or bury him six-feet under, but he wouldn't shoot her. The anguish he'd seen in her furrowed brow tightened his chest while the determined set of her shoulders earned his respect. Neither would allow him to pull the trigger.

Ryan sidled up to the wall, twisted the knob, and shoved the door wide. He thought he'd prepared for everything. Taking cover behind the mound of bodies, if she started shooting. Bum-rushing her, if she tried to attack. Tossing her over his shoulder and carrying her out, if she refused to come willingly. But fuck it all. He had not prepared for tears. Not from any woman. Most especially not from the badass who had gotten the drop on him.

Each gut-rending sob punched him square in the chest, bypassed his sternum, and landed on his heart. He eased around the corner and immediately wished his typical flight instinct had kicked in at the first sign of a female's tears. She huddled in a ball much like the one he'd found her hunched in at the makeshift jail. Only worse. Her fists knitted against her chest and she curled into herself. Her head hung low. The hiccupped breaths she fought for shook her entire body.

He'd never frozen on the job, until now. His synapses fired on ultra slow-mo speed. The lead in his feet weighed more than a team of horses could budge. Impotence bathed him. Not for the first time. But for the first time with a beautiful woman at his feet. The only way he knew to help required her legs spread and his face buried between them. With this hellcat, it didn't seem like the wisest course of action. And it wouldn't get them to extraction any faster.

His watch told him to grab her and run like his shoes were on fire. He stepped into the room. Reluctantly his gaze left her, traveling to the computer screen. The shipment roster no longer clung to the bright glow. In its place, the main filing system stuck to the screen with nearly thirty documents and spreadsheets stacked open behind the file icons.

"It's time to go," he whispered.

"Then go." She contrasted his quiet tone with a vicious yell.

Their gazes tangled, preventing his escape. In the depths of bronze flecks he saw a desperation he understood more than most. Despite his wide smiles and friendly banter, he knew hell by the prick of its serrated mountain range, the burn of its lava lakes, the sting of its acrid air in his lungs. She knew its topography too.

"I'm not leaving without you."

Her hand slapped at the tears streaming her cheeks. The laugh that spewed from her lips matched that of a man he'd once visited in an asylum. Its hysterical notes punctuated the precariousness of their situation. "Men. No matter how different, you're all the same. If I'd been some troll-looking woman or an old man, you wouldn't feel any moral compunction about putting a bullet in my head or simply turning around and walking away."

Ryan knew it wasn't true, but her words had him cataloguing past missions and second-guessing himself. "Maybe the men you're used to dealing with, but not me. So, you have ten seconds to decide whether you're leaving on your own two feet or slung over my shoulder."

Iron rod steeled her backbone once more and all traces of sadness fled. Her eyes narrowed and her lips pinched to white lines. "I'm not leaving."

Ryan started toward her. "Six. Seven. Eight..."

She scrambled to her feet, the chain rattling in the rush. "Not until the next shipment arrives."

Well, she put the words where they'd do the most damage. Right in his festered unease about leaving the next group to their fates. He stopped three, four feet from her, this time ready for an attack. "You mean the shipment that has a detail of at least ten armed guards?"

"I'll take my chances."

"You'll die."

"People do it everyday." She gestured to the corpse to his left.

"Yeah. Some people need killing."

"And Émile Gabrone is one of those people."

"You're not staying just to kill Gabrone." Though he had no idea what it was, he saw a plan —more intricate than suicide for the sake of revenge—twinkling in her eyes.

"Nope." Her brow knit ever tighter in defiance.

He smiled at her dogged determination and gruff manner. "Why stay?"

From its pool on the floor to the cuff on her wrist, the metal swayed as she balled her fists. "I need information, and thanks to you all my leads are dead."

Ryan gripped her forearm and held her bloody wrist high between them. "Your captors are dead."

She recoiled an inch from his growled retort, but rebounded faster than an MBA All-Star. "They caught me because I wanted them to."

"Son of a bitch. They claimed all sites clear. Are you compromised? Burned?"

"I'm not CIA."

"Then who the hell are you?" He took a step closer to emphasize the importance of his question.

"I'm Piper," she said with a venom-sweet smile.

Ryan dropped his head several inches, leveling his gaze with hers. "Not what I meant."

She bit the inside of her cheek and shook her head back and forth so long he thought she'd gone mute on him again. "Former L.A.P.D."

"You're a long way from home."

"And you're a fucking genius."

"Aren't you a charmer." Ryan tugged her alongside him and headed for the door. She pulled against his hold, but didn't fight as much as he knew she could.

"I'm not leaving," she growled.

"No, *we're* not, but we are going to get that damn cuff off your wrist and take care of your cuts."

Chapter Seven

"No dead bodies?" Piper arched a brow and made a show of peering around the chunky wood island and the table nestled in the breakfast nook. "I'm amazed."

"Keep on pushing me. I could add another." Ryan deposited the first aid kit he'd snagged from the hallway bathroom and narrowed his gaze at her.

"No, you couldn't."

"Cocky aren't you?"

"Confident. *You're* cocky." She dropped her gaze to his crotch. Her head tilted and her thin lips pursed.

"Here I was trying to be gentlemanly and discreet. You stomp all over tradition, don't you?"

"Meaning?"

He crooked a finger at her. "Come here before you get angry and try breaking my nose again."

"You might want to check it. I see blood and a hump at the base."

"The hump is courtesy of the last guy who tried and succeeded. The blood will wash away."

"All of it?" Her lips formed a grim line. "Seems you have a penchant for taking lives."

"I have a duty. Now get over here," he snapped.

When she didn't budge, he jangled the keys he'd confiscated from one of the dead men along the way. Piper curbed her urge to stomp her feet like an agitated bull. She settled for a huff, crossed the kitchen, and offered him her cuff.

"You chose a male-dominated profession in one of the toughest precincts in the States. If you're ever in distress, there's no damsel in it. Just one pissed lady. You've probably never needed a man for anything. Not even to get you off. And you'd probably spit in any guy's face who had the cajones to ask for your hand in marriage."

He was already too damn close to the mark, to her body. The thick pads of his fingers warmed her forearm, while his eyes warmed her everywhere else.

"Who was dumb enough to hurt you? Father? Lover?"

Piper snapped her jaw closed the moment she realized the damn thing dangled open like an anglerfish on the hunt. She snatched the keys from his blood-crusted hands and green-stained fingers. He let her retreat to the other side of the island without a word. She longed to turn away from his knowing gaze. The azure-blue orbs with their reflective, nearly white flecks saw too much and reflected back her flaws.

Pinning the latch to the counter with her wrist and hip, Piper unlocked the crude accessory, removed her arm, and watched the heavy links tug from the shiny surface. It *thwacked* atop the pile. Freedom lightened her mood and body like the Lord above flipped a switch. Piper raised her chin.

"No one has ever hurt me. Not a father or lover.

"My dad was donor number 489760 from The Sperm Bank of California. I've never needed a man for anything. Neither did my mother, who raised three daughters on her own. I like men to get me off. I just don't like them to hang around long after."

His head canted and his studying eyes shone bright, surrounded by the dull gray and green of combat paint. Piper mapped the contours of his face. His wide-muscled jaw. The depression of dimples below his high cheeks and the lickable one at the brunt of his chin. Lips thicker than her own. A gently sloping brow pinched in thought. And damn that smile. She'd only seen a flash of it and knew she couldn't take any more.

Sure, the stranger was crazy handsome, but something below the All-American exterior pulled her deep. A quiet pain hid behind his blinding smile. When he turned away and stepped to the sink, Piper released the breath she hadn't noticed she'd been holding. He turned the water to steaming and went to work rolling the sleeves of his BDU's. With copious amounts of soap he scrubbed the paint and life force of several men from his hands.

But damn, she couldn't rip her gaze from his forearms. Tanned skin stretched over fibrous cords of muscle stacked in a thick pile. A pathway of veins coursed over them and disappeared beneath his cuffed sleeve. Most surprising of all was the thatch of golden blond hair sprinkling the expanse. She hadn't paid much attention to the hair slicked atop his head. Now she saw the blackness for what it was, black grease to hide the shine of his boyishly light hair.

When he called her over with a tilt of his head she moved her ass, unprepared for another battle or to see those arms in action. The roller coaster of emotions over the last thirty minutes left her bone weary. As she cleared the island, her steps slowed and renewed energy coursed through her body. Saliva pooled in her mouth, better used exploring his body. The lips of her sex bloomed an invitation. The beat of her heart accelerated to the point of pain. Every gauge in her body blinked red. Warning. Danger. Run. Never before had she approached a man who saw through her as though she were his personal looking glass.

He held a clean, tanned hand out for her injury. Her eyes riveted on thick scar tissue bisecting the girth of his palm. It splayed like a red spider, a lump at the center with fissures sprawling in nearly every direction. She found his gaze and stilled her hand inches from his.

"It's okay."

Piper didn't know what he referred to, but the reassurance gave her the muster to move again. Before she could stop herself, the tips of her fingers skimmed the dune of pink marring his wide, callused hand. She slid along the scar until it ran over the edge and their palms met in an intimate handshake.

The shock of contact reverberated around the room like the concussive waves of detonation. His Adam's apple bobbed on a deep swallow, telling her he felt it too. The pad of his thumb danced over the back of her hand. Her nerve endings wept at the tenderness. The heat she could handle, but the care speared too close to the center of her heart.

"I can't...I can clean it myself," she fumbled.

He tugged her against his side. "You're right handed and probably wouldn't clean it well enough to stave off infection. It'd be a shame to lose your shooting hand."

"It hasn't gotten infected yet."

"How long has it been like this?"

"Two months. Give or take a couple of weeks."

The pack of weapons and ammo strapped to his torso gave a few inches of cushion. Still, the closeness pinged out her sensors, until he put her wrist under the water. The irritating sting she'd lived with over the course of her captivity was a gnat bite compared to this rattlesnake strike. Her eyes watered of their own volition. She tried to blink the tears away, but the bastards rolled down her cheek.

"How'd you manage to keep it clean for so long?"

"Gabrone took care of me."

"I'll bet he did." The words growled from his throat.

"Not like that. He had a weird fixation and wanted me willingly. He didn't want anyone else to have me either. It worked to my advantage."

"What's an LA cop doing in the middle of a Mexican cartel's human trafficking ring?" The slanted gaze he flashed over his shoulder ruffled her already disheveled feathers.

"I'm not dirty, if that's what your expression implies."

Ryan placed her raw wrist back under the flowing water and scrubbed.

"Son of a *puta. Que te den.*" She screamed the insults and clamped onto the thick base of his bicep with her free hand.

"If you keep talking like that, when I'm done here I'll have to scrub your mouth out."

Piper clamped her lips between her teeth and howled at the ceiling. When she ran out of breath she refueled. "Sadomasochist."

"I take no pleasure in your pain. Or my own." His gaze found hers then dropped to his arm where her nails bit into his skin. "But I have enjoyed your gyrating hips." His dimple flashed before he turned and got back to work.

Focusing on her breathing and not moving a muscle, Piper survived the next thirty seconds by force of will. Ryan turned off the water, stepped back, and revealed her hot-pink wrist. She looked as though she had a raw strip steak for a bracelet. Very unfashionable. Very disgusting.

"Hold it up and don't touch it." He turned to the first aid kit and pulled out several packages of gauze, tape, and salve. "I'm sorry it hurt, but I had to remove all the dead skin. I'll change your bandage again tomorrow, before we go to war.

"Are you prepared for it? Because that's what it's going to be—an all-out battle. You and me against all of them. Plus, we have twenty or more innocents to keep out of harm's way." A long exhale curved the edge of his mouth into a frown and his gaze returned to hers. "If the Sinaloa use them as shields, if they all die, can you handle it?"

Piper couldn't answer. Was she willing to risk twenty lives for one? Her mind said, "No." But her fissured heart said, "Yes." And for once, her heart would win out over her head. Ryan's hand warmed the sensitive skin under her bicep as he pulled her toward him. They stood imbued in silence, mingling uneasy breaths.

Caught in his heat, her lips fell open in wild invitation and waited. Her momentarily reckless heart galloped behind her breasts. She longed for him to yank her against the hard metal weaponry strapped to his chest. To seize her mouth with his own painted lips. To smudge the already spent camouflage over her face and neck. To make her forget it all for a little while.

His searing gaze alighted on her mouth and he pulled her closer still. The other hand spread across the column of her neck, heating through to her aching core. His fingers skated up her keen flesh, burning a path over the ledge of her chin. The pad of his thumb swept across her top lip then into the wet edge of her lower on its way back.

He nestled his scarred palm behind her ear and burrowed his fingers in her hair. His powerful hand aligned their gazes and his lips fell open. "The absence of something, a father, a lover, doesn't mean it can't hurt you."

Piper struggled at his gut-twisting words, pushing against the hulking rounds of his shoulders with all her might. His hands twisted in her hair and firmed on her arm in a latch similar to that of a mating lion. Her nipples peaked beneath the fabric of her cotton tank, and she hated her traitorous body as much as the man inciting the reaction.

"Shhh," he crooned.

Her chest heaved in pants that soaked her panties through and left her light headed. But her struggle ceased at his easy command. His gaze roved her face, burned her chest, and caressed her shorts-clad legs. The muscles in his neck and jaw flexed, and his nostrils flared in an unmistakable sign of lust. She couldn't see past his full vest, but his hard length, cuddled against the joint of her thighs, made her wish she could speak to beg.

He tugged her head forward and rested his forehead against hers. "I don't know what you're after, but if you look at me like that again, you're going to get something you've not bargained for. My fuck em' and flee days are over and my true sexual proclivities require your total surrender. Something I doubt you're willing to give."

His exhale washed over her breasts, making her wish she were capable of such yielding. But her mother hadn't raised her to cow to anyone, especially a man. Sierra Vega taught her to fight for what she wanted. To hold her head up through a storm. To never lose sight of what was important in life. Family.

"Tomorrow we'll set up an ambush that will keep the people safe. So, unless you can see yourself on your knees before me with your head bowed, after I bandage your wrist, I suggest you go to the first bedroom upstairs, shower, and sleep. We have a couple of long days ahead of us."

Chapter Eight

Mark that shit down in a record book.

Never in his life had Ryan sent a wildly beautiful and willing woman from his arms. But fuck, he owed it to himself to get what he needed from a relationship. Cold couplings with women who didn't possess the strength to handle his desire were a thing of the past. His days of club play were behind him too. The Dungeon had satisfied part of his need, but left him as cool as the others in the end. Too bad the woman slamming stuff around in the room over his head wasn't relationship or submission ready. She stirred a protective instinct inside him that boggled his mind and balls.

Ryan pulled the satphone from his ruck and dialed Base. "Sierra. Hotel. Echo. Papa. Hotel. Echo. Romeo. Delta. One. Nine. Nine. Six."

After a series of beeps, an operator answered. "Voice confirmation complete. Agent Noble, how may I direct your call?"

"Commander Tucker, please."

"What's wrong?" Tucker answered.

"Extraction's blown."

"Are you injured?"

"No."

"Compromised?"

"No, but I'd like to be."

"Spill it, Noble."

"They had a prisoner. An a—"

"Put Ruez in interrogation. And check our other teams." Though he'd covered the phone with his hand, Tucker's holler filled the line. The connection rustled again. "The place is supposed to be clean for two weeks."

"She's American. An unusual case. Former L.A.P.D. Allowed herself to be caught for information. I need to know what she's after."

"Name?"

"Piper is all I have so far. There's something else." Ryan's thumb increased its beat on the end of the magazine at the front of his pack.

"No shit," Tucker huffed. "Otherwise, you'd have tossed her on your back and made it to the damn HELO as ordered."

"Yes, sir. They're expecting a shipment Monday. We'll need on-site extraction for thirty-five at 0400" Shit, he hated disappointing people. But the truth was, if he'd left the shipment, the people, behind, he'd have disappointed himself more. So, he had Piper to thank for this misadventure.

"I'll send Khani on the Chinook with a couple of old friends. But you know I can't give you on site pick-up. I'm squashing too many international laws as it is. All I can give is five miles from the coast. Your drop location."

"Yes, sir."

Over the next two hours Ryan poured his angst and agitation into cleanup. He stuffed the seven bodies scattered about the house into the Suburban in the garage. The three at the perimeter he propped-up inside the Jeep since they'd be "on guard" when the cargo arrived in the wee hours of the morning. He took special care wrapping the seatbelt across Big 'Un's chest and around his neck. Before heading inside he closed the door to

Piper's prison and scooped the broken handle from the dirt. He molded the metal in his hand and hoped they'd make it stateside without a small metal box.

Chapter Nine

Piper twirled a damp lock of hair and peered through the slit of the vinyl blinds. Ryan jostled the knob he'd broken off the guesthouse in his palm. His hard, tender, far too welcoming palm. At least this time those hands didn't carry a dead body. He turned with the handle in tow. A slow, sexy saunter swayed his hips. Her body warmed in appreciation. She found herself on tiptoes as he neared the porch and obscurity. A step from it, he stopped, lifted his chin, and touched two fingers to his brow before disappearing into the house.

"Shit. Pure stealth, Vega."

She tossed the gentle curl over her shoulder and let her finger fall from the window dressing. Her ears pricked at the vibration from the closing door and the tread of his heavy boots through the living room. He wanted her to know where he was. Earlier he hadn't made a whisper until the knock resonated on the bathroom door. She hadn't heard his retreat either. Only the shoes Gabrone confiscated from her upon capture, sitting outside the steaming room, proved he'd been there at all.

The footfalls rumbled up the stairs, and her heart stood at attention along with her nipples. She tried pressing the offending flesh down, but only aggravated the problem. His treads died just outside her door and Piper wondered if she could submit to a man, just in the bedroom, just once. Her breath quieted in her lungs as she waited for his knock.

Moments collected then overflowed, forcing her to take a breath or pass out. Her hands rung the hem of the oversize T-shirt she'd taken from the closet. Finally her reserve broke. Piper rushed to the door and grabbed the handle. She hoped he'd be there, but fully expected he'd swung past to check on her then spirited away as he'd done before.

She wrenched the knob from the frame and skidded to a halt, her hair fanning out over her shoulders before swinging back against her sensitive, cotton-covered breasts. A smile quirked his mouth and suddenly a blush of foolishness heated her cheeks. The son of a bitch had waited intentionally, making her come to him. Not that he had that kind of power over her. She'd come because she wanted to. Plain and simple. She wanted to see him again. And now that she did, her brain short-circuited.

The ammunitions pack, assault riffle, ruck, and BDU top all hung from his left hand. A desert-brown tee stretched to accommodate his sinewy torso, pulling taut over his wide shoulders and full chest before tapering to his waist, clinging to every defined abdominal muscle. Sweat dripped from his chin, soaking the already drenched material.

"Since you're still awake..." The hollow of his dimple grew and she wanted to slam the door in his self-assured face.

When he didn't continue she hollered, "What? Since I'm still awake, what?"

He bit his lip. The smile he gave was an all-out assault on her self-preservation. "I was hoping you'd stand watch while I grab a shower."

It was all she could do to keep from sputtering, 'No, *I'd rather sit on your face and rub that smirk off of it.*' Damn the smile and the man. He sure knew how to bring a girl to her knees. Instead, she said, "Sure. Not like I'll be sleeping anytime soon anyway."

"Here. Do you know how to use this?" He lifted an AK-47 from the door jam and handed it over.

"Yeah, you want me to show you?"

"Nah. You have a malevolent little gleam in your eye and I'd prefer my middle not look like a sieve." He stepped back and turned down the corridor. "Your window perch is a great look-out spot. I don't expect company, but let me know the moment you even think you see something. Oh, and here." He pulled a monocular from his pack and tossed it. "Nice catch."

"I can juggle too. I'm here all night. Don't forget to leave a tip."

"You keep pushing me and I'll give you a tip, all right." His blue eyes flashed white-hot before he turned and continued down the hall.

Piper guessed he was talking about the tip of his cock. That notion combined with the rippled view of his cloth-covered back flushed her cheeks sauna hot. How dare he leave her scorching and far past bothered? She stomped back inside the room and slammed the door. Before the wood quit shuddering, she turned the lock. A lock wouldn't keep him out, but it would send a message. She took up post at her eagle's nest and dared any of those sons-of-bitches to show their face.

He took the longest shower in the history of man. And her mind's eye had no problem picturing him sluicing the dirt from swollen muscles or taking pleasures with his own body. She'd worked herself into a fuckable frenzy by the time she heard his boots on the tile floor. He paused in front of her bedroom. With anticipation slicked hands she set the night-vision field glass on the floor and rested the gun against the wall at the window before turning toward the strip of light seeping beneath the door.

"Get some sleep," he barked, and then shuffled down the stairs.

"Seriously? Not even a, 'Hey have you given any thought to that whole submission thing 'cause I've got a boner the size of California you could practice with.' Fuck."

Piper fell face-first onto the mattress and growled. After expelling all the air from her lungs, she crawled to the top and pummeled the pillow in a two-fold endeavor. Comfort and stress release. She curled into a ball atop the covers and tried to relish the soft mattress under her body and the oblivion of dark. For whatever reason, the prison light stayed on twenty-four hours a day, seven days a week. The incessant light had been more difficult to adapt to than the absent bed, and even the loss of freedom. But those had only been bearable because her imprisonment had a purpose. One the commando fucked with military precision.

Chapter Ten

Aryanna Noble's serene and youthfully smooth face screwed tighter with each failed call. Her blue eyes met his and she smiled like a scarecrow. "Can you think of anyone else she'd visit?" Ryan could only shake his head. "A boy maybe? Oh, the Tuckers moved in next to Holly and they have a very handsome older son. Maybe they went to spy on him. I'll try her house again."

Blood pumped through Ryan's veins like it was trying to escape. Like if it pumped fast enough it could flee his body and the nightmares plaguing him.

His mother inhaled through her nose and released a long breath and struggled to remain calm through her futile attempts to track her daughter's whereabouts. His pre-pubescent whine droned, "Why'd we have to cancel the party? The goal's ready and everything. All we needed was the cake. I hope Becca gets grounded forever."

"Because your sister has been missing for three hours!" As the shrill words left her mouth the sky clouded. Lifeless gray overtook streaks of sunshine. Fat rain droplets pelted his face, soaked through his clothes. Ryan turned toward the house, but stopped short. His mom lay in a huddled ball on the concrete drive, sobbing. "No! Why? Rebecca!" The policemen stood over her, offering inadequate support.

God, he hated these dreams. Hated the distorted memories. No matter what he did, they never stopped. Every night his regret visited in one grizzly version or another. And, though he knew they weren't real, he couldn't seem to wake until the end.

Like every time before, his dad arrived in an all-out run, staring over Ryan's head as if he didn't exist. The man's hair silvered as he skid on slick bottom wing-tips to his wife's side. Only it wasn't his wife anymore.

U.S. Senator Jake Noble rolled the limp body into his arms. Long blonde hair cascaded from his sister's gaunt visage. Death-hazed eyes stared back. Lightning stained the sky a brilliant white and the rumble called forth a rain of bullets that peppered Rebecca's body with hundreds of irreparable holes and their lives with hopelessness.

The scream he heaved in the dream never followed him into consciousness. Otherwise, they'd put him in an institution. But he could never escape the churn of his gut or the quake of his heart. Ryan leapt into reality and from the chair he used as a bed. Morning light filled the room, illuminating the barrel of his sidearm centered between Piper's bite-sized breasts.

"Hey, I offered to cook you brunch, not make you have sex the old fashioned way." Feet spread a comfortable shoulder's width apart and hips slung to one side, she flashed him a smile. "I never cook. So, you should jump at the offer." The thumb on her left hand hung on the belt loop of dark jeans. They contrasted with the fluffy white gauze wrapped around her wrist, dangling mid-thigh.

Ryan straightened as though he'd been electrocuted. The H&K fell to his side, and he rubbed the horror and sleep from his eyes. A strand of tears tumbled onto his bare chest. The moisture blended with the sheen of sweat and took cover in the bristle of his hair. Maybe she wouldn't notice the first tears he'd shed since his sister's funeral.

He wiped the remnants on the boxers he'd borrowed from a dead man. Probably wouldn't have to give them back, since the guy wouldn't need them anymore. His chin raised and he breathed until his lungs couldn't hold a molecule more. He released the breath through parted lips. The technique pulled the reins on his erratic panting and wild heart. He'd had so much practice pulling himself together after an episode, it only took one more breath before he could speak.

"Or maybe I should cook. Cooking, like sex, gets better with practice and discipline."

Her copper eyes tilted toward the ceiling and her cinched braid waggled with the shake of her head. "If I liked pussy, my life would be so much easier." With that nugget, she turned on the soles of her tan leather boots and headed for the kitchen.

A smile quirked Ryan's lips despite the stains on his insides. He shoved his feet into thieved jeans, yanked them up his legs, then pulled a white tee over his head. Gun tucked neatly into the small of his back, he turned to the window and surveyed the horizon by day. Too bad the Sinaloa weren't scheduled to arrive until the black hours of the morning. He'd be able to see them coming from any direction for two miles. As he knew all too well, the thin brush, scrawny cacti, and rocky terrain didn't provide much cover. He had thermal and night vision monoculars, but nothing beat daylight.

He turned his back on the monochromatic rainbow of brown and followed his nose. The thing led him to the curves of Piper's ass peeking out from behind the refrigerator door. On the island, a cutting board held a whole avocado and beheaded tomato, playing host to the partially imbedded blade. Pans cluttered the stove. One sizzled with eggs while another frothed bubbles over the edge. The third spat grease with a loud pop.

"Mierda."

"You need some help?"

She closed the stainless-steel door with her foot and turned away as if he hadn't said a word. The overflowing contents of her arms spilled onto the counter. She plucked a tortilla from a paper bag and tossed it into the popping oil. The white round shimmied in the pan while she whipped a tea bag from the pile and dropped it into the water. She turned the burner off and slid it to a free one.

With a frying pan handle in each palm she shook loose the eggs and tortilla and flipped them into the air. After catching and returning them to the fire, she turned, lips pursed and hands propped on her hips. "You can set the table."

"Set the table? I plan to blow this place to the moon in a few hours, and you want me to set the table?"

"Yes, as in plates, forks, knives, napkins, cups." She sliced the tomato and cored the avocado so quickly Ryan found his brow pulled low. "Help, if you're going to. Everything will be ready in two minutes."

Ryan hustled around the kitchen, pulling open most of the cabinets and drawers in his search of the requested items. Two by two he set them on the lacquered table across from one another. Before he finished with the flatware, Piper ushered over two plates full of food. She swirled around, snagging a pitcher of orange juice from the island.

Taking a calculated risk, Ryan pulled out her chair and offered it with a wave of his hand. Surprisingly, he didn't pull back a nub. Amazingly, she sat without a hint of sass.

"Provecho," she bowed.

"Provecho."

Her gaze followed the fork to his lips and her brow arched. Taste exploded in his mouth as hot and as vivid as the woman sitting in front of him. The creamy avocado and sweet tomato countered the spice of the eggs. Ryan placed his hand over his heart. "I'll admit, I'm wrong about the practice. Either you have it or you don't. And you sure as hell have it."

She gifted him with a flash of her pearly whites. "I may be rusty, but I've had more than my fair share of practice."

"Are we talking cooking or sex now?"

"Cooking, but..." she said with a shrug. "It could apply to both, I suppose."

"Who did you cook for, Piper?"

Her tongue slid over her upper lip, stealing away a bit of fluffy green. She took another bite and followed it with a swig of juice. "My little sister, who's not so little anymore."

"Hence, the not cooking?"

"Yeah," she agreed.

He remained quiet, hoping she'd fill the void with words. She considered him with a tilt of her head and as much intent as he studied her. They ate in silence, measuring one another. Once her plate sat empty, she wiped her mouth.

"My mother worked a lot when we were young." A hint of a smile arched her lips. "So, I took care of dinner and bedtime."

"Just you and your sister?"

"Ivy," she supplied. "No, my grandmother lived with us, but rose and slept with the sun. And napped with the cat." Her eyes darted in the corners of her mind for a moment. He guessed gauging how much to say. That penny-shine gaze settled back on his hair momentarily before meeting his gaze. "My older sister lived with us too. Technically. But she enjoyed the freedom our mother's absence provided."

"Another reason you're so hell bent on doing everything yourself?" Ryan kicked back in the seat.

Piper's lips thinned and her face screwed tight for a five count. She shoved her plate to the side and slowly relaxed. "Could be. Is your nightmare a one-off thing?"

"No."

"PTSD?"

"It's not PTSD."

All malfeasance fled her face and her fingers spread wide on the wooden table. Though a table separated their proximity, the weight of her stare pinned him in place. "You think because you're a bad-ass you can't get it? A cop on the force, a damn fine officer, got pinned down. Even though he read those bastards their rights and shoved them in jail, he had nightmares every time he slept about one of the bullets ripping him apart. He never made anything of it. Less than a year after, he killed himself."

"You think I'm a badass?" he asked.

Piper rolled her eyes.

"Fine," he surrendered, "I don't think a person can get PTSD at age ten."

Ryan shot from the table and collected the plates. He rinsed them under the heavy flow, focusing far too long on a defect in the blue glaze. Piper's hand hooked his bicep. He pivoted his head in her direction and his heart dropped into his shoes. The rich tan of her skin was cast with a chalky glow and her bottom lip quivered.

He slammed the lever, cutting off the water, and searched the room for the cause of her distress. When he didn't see anything he strained his sensitive hearing for any unfamiliar noise. Her shaking head stopped him.

"You were ten and it still affects you?"

Women, he didn't understand them farther than he could lick them front to back. "What's wrong, Piper? It's not like I'm going to swallow a bullet and leave you to deal with this mess on your own."

"I know." She nodded. "I just...I can't imagine..."

"It's fine. I'm fine." He shrugged off her touch and walked into the living room. He used surveillance as an excuse, hurrying out onto the front patio. Piper followed and skirted through the arched door before he closed it. She stepped away, walking several feet before leaning against the wall, her long legs kicked out and crossed at the ankle. Like she intended to stay as long as it took.

He shifted his face toward the horizon, but saw nothing. The past, present, and future tormented him, but no more so than did her presence. He couldn't ignore her. Lord knows, he tried.

"You really want to know?"

"Yes," she whispered.

Crossing his arms, he turned to face her. "Well, there are some things I really want to know too."

Her chin wagged in denial before he finished the sentence. Her lips parted, but the words evaporated in the dry air before reaching his ears.

Piper clamped her strong jaw closed and her lids followed suit.

"You may not need anyone's help, but it doesn't mean it wouldn't benefit your cause."

Her head rested back against the adobe and her chest heaved, drawing his gaze to her engorged nipples. He turned back to the land. He wished away his hard-on. When it didn't leave on its own he chased it away with memories.

"Nearly eighteen years ago my parents surprised me after breakfast pancakes with a ten-foot hoop. I begged them non-stop to construct the thing. Of course, my father had to go into the office for a few hours. Even on the special Saturday. Leaving my mom to decorate the house, cook, and build the goal for my party.

"Did you ever see the movie *Space Jam*?"

"Only a thousand times. Ivy ate only vegetables and she swore she was Bugs Bunny. She wore construction paper ears and a cotton ball tail so much my mom bought stock in Crayola and Cotton."

"Make sure they have Michael Jordan and Bugs Bunny on the cake and don't mess it up." Ryan propped his palms on the wooden railing and spread his feet. "That was the last thing I said to my sister. For the first time after getting her license my mom let her drive without an adult in the car. Rebecca only smiled at my demands." His grip bit into the finish.

"She was car-jacked. But the son of a bitch wasn't satisfied. Tried to take her jewelry. She fought back and he emptied the magazine into her chest."

"It's not your fault," Piper said.

"She probably thought he was trying to force her into the car. And who really knows. Maybe he was."

"It's not your fault," Piper repeated.

He'd been so wrapped up in a basketball goal that rusted through without ever being used, and a cake that never left the bakery, for a party that never happened, that he hadn't waved his sister goodbye or even blown her a kiss. "I know."

"In your head you know, but in your heart... guilt bores holes so deep. You could fall forever and never hit the bottom. Purgatory with your heart slammed against the back of your chest. Your throat mangled raw from the scream that won't stop. A train of what if's running the same track in your mind, but refusing you the sweet relief of derailment. Of severing your brain stem and ending the shame."

Her words shot an arrow dead center down one of the chasms in his heart. Ryan pried his clenched fingers from the railing, and then turned. The hole must not have been all that deep. The broad-head found purchase at the cinched lips and rivulets flowing from Piper's closed eyes. Agony— hers, his—sliced through his chest, razing every naked nerve ending on its sojourn.

Chapter Eleven

The rasp of his breath drew nearer. Piper retreated inside herself. Blindness her only protection against his knowing stare. Somehow this stranger reached deep inside and poked at a place she'd cordoned off and tried desperately to obliterate from her consciousness. His incessant nudges ached like mental images of the first homicide she worked. It brought pain, immediate and sharp, but somehow lessened the torment. Lessened the fear of the misery to come.

No way would she acknowledge it.

"Sounds like you've studied contrition intimately." His deep voice rumbled and the warmth of his breath tickled her neck.

Piper held completely still, waiting for him to leave.

His touch settled at the corner of her eye. The weight of it pressed firm before trailing to her ear and off the edge of her bare lobe, taking her tears with it.

In a battle of wills, Piper never lost. Then again, she'd never lost her will. Until craving overcame determination. Winning took a backseat. Independence hopped in next to it. Desire gripped the wheel with both hands and opened the throttle. Her eyes opened. Her chin dropped to scope their fill.

Gone was the greasy gorilla he'd been last night. In his place a shocker stood. With his floppy blond hair and wholesome good looks, he could easily shoulder a Ralph Lauren campaign. The white-fire eyes could melt the habit off Sister Irene at Our Lady of Sorrow. Or scare the piss out of a world-class criminal. He truly was a conundrum of a man.

Ryan threw a leg over her crossed ones, nesting them in the V of his. The move brought his lips a breath away. Piper wished for the instincts she had the last time he got this close.

"Why can't you have regular sex?" Before she could stop the thought it fell out of her mouth.

His jaw lowered and his gaze peeked from beneath his thick brows. "You trying to change the subject?"

"I sincerely wish."

"I can and have had regular sex, Miss...?" His dimples winked in a burdened smirk.

"Vega," she whispered.

"Piper Vega, regular sex is mundane. Mediocre at best." He shrugged.

"Maybe you just haven't done it with the right person." She inhaled, stuffing her lungs full of his masculine scent, and enjoyed the hit. Like a pothead discovering crystal meth, she was hooked. Whether she liked it or not.

"No doubt. But what I'm talking about, if done right, blows regular sex out of the water every single time."

"What makes you think you can do it right?"

"I can't." Ryan's thumb mimicked the earlier caress over her left cheek. "*We* could." He placed the pad between his lips and sucked off the moisture. "It's a trust so absolute I could aim a gun to your head. Smile. Pull the trigger. Kill the man sneaking up behind you. And all the while you'd smile back at me. Never for an instant believing I could harm a strand of your hair. An inch of your skin. A piece of your heart."

His palm lay against her thudding chest.

"It's making love and never knowing where the next touch will fall. Never knowing how heartbreakingly gentle. How passionate. How rigid it will be. The shock of orgasm pulls you under the wave you never saw coming. It wrestles you to the point of exhaustion and allows you to breathe only when you've died *la petite mort*. When you've given all and received everything in return."

Piper swore her vagina magnetized. Her hips tilted and surged forward, sparking contact with his steely erection. Her breath caught as she anticipated his next move. Would he subdue her with a kiss and plastic cuffs? Would he bind her to the chair he'd slept in and devour her body tit to toe? She didn't know, but her nerves rattled with the eagerness to find out.

Ryan's head lolled back and his thick chest expanded, molding the ridge of his torso to the cotton. On exhale he groaned like a bear ready to bash in a car door for its snack. An electric thrill shot up her spine. Her lips parted in preparation. The pressure at her chest increased. Her back flattened against the wall. Their gazes locked.

"Come on. We have a hell of a lot of work to do before the Sinaloa arrive." His hand dropped. He stepped back and turned toward the door.

"Asshole," she hollered. Piper would have scraped her jaw off the ground, but it was too tense in rage. Rage at herself, mostly.

"Yep. But not usually," he said. Hand on the knob, he gestured her inside the house.

"What, I bring out the worst in you?" She sashayed into the compound, but avoided looking into his eyes.

"My old partner would say you bring out my best."

"So, you're gay?"

A full belly laugh assailed her ears and made her glad her back was to him. She stomped into the kitchen and rounded the island, but didn't raise her gaze until the threat of his dimples waned.

"Let's just make a plan and forget everything else. All I want to do is get these people out of here safely."

"All?"

"No," she said with a wobble of her head that would have earned her a whipping from her momma back in the day. "I want to kill these bastards too."

Ryan's smile compressed into a line. He scrubbed the heel of his hand across his forehead and flipped back some wayward strands. "Killing is not an easy thing."

"When you've seen what I've seen...it is." Piper flattened her hands on the wood and leaned forward. "Chained to the wall, unable to help at all, two shipments came through here. If it had been drugs or weapons, maybe I couldn't take their lives. But I've looked into the eyes of these girls. I've see their freedom ripped from them under the guise of hope. I've seen the promise of their future. Its forced prostration, multiple forced abortions, and an early death. A death that they'll welcome with wide arms."

"I'm putting my life in your hands, Piper. If your law-abiding conscience gets the best of you, don't leave me pissin' in the wind."

"I was a cop, Ryan. Not a saint."

Those cursed dimples caught her off guard. "What?" she barked.

He shook his head. His gaze shifted to the window through which she spied the garage. "I know the convoy usually has a lead car, the bus with the cargo, and two tails. But where do they go when they arrive?"

"I've only seen the bus parked outside the door. But what I've pieced together is the lead car goes to the garage, the first tail stays with the bus, and the last pulls to the front of the house."

"And where's Gabrone during all this?"

Piper pulled back and shifted her weight to her right foot. She slapped the braid over her shoulder and contemplated her answer. Not knowing what he'd plan, she couldn't yet weigh her options. "In the last car."

"You sure about that?" He rubbed his knuckles across the stubble sprouting on his chin.

"Yeah."

"All right. How many in each car? Best guess."

"Two up front. Three in the backseat. If things are running hot with another cartel, they'll ride two in the hatch. "

"That's twenty-one armed men, plus how many in the bus?"

"Just the driver."

"Seriously?"

"They're hauling thirty girls into the middle of nowhere, most of whom aren't a day over seventeen, surrounded by men ready to fuck them or shoot them. The guys don't exactly have to worry about an uprising of unarmed, terrified women."

"Point taken." His sun-bleached locks ruffled with his nod. "So, I'll re-wire the garage to blow on one detonator, rig the front entrance on another, and I'll take the bus driver and lead car."

"But Gabrone...is in the tail car," she stuttered.

"And you want him dead, right?"

He offered up a palm and one shoulder shrug.

"Yes," she conceded.

"Nothing like a couple of globs of C-4 to do the job."

"Fine, but do you think you can take, what, eight guys by yourself? Why not blow them to smithereens too?"

"Too close to the bus, the people we're trying to protect."

A chill nearly frosted the hairs on Piper's arm. She'd worked hostage situations before, but as a beat cop. Her only responsibility had been keeping the onlookers from interfering. And now she was responsible for taking out two carloads of bad guys and the well-being of so many scared and confused girls. What if it all went wrong? What if they all died because of her? What if Ryan bled out on the dusty ground?

"Hey?"

His gaze roamed her arms, which she chaffed with the ineffective cups of her palms. He stepped around the bar, wrapped his hot fingers around her uninjured wrist, and tugged her close. Against her better judgment, Piper allowed him to envelope her in his heat.

Yesterday his gear provided an adequate barrier against body contact. Today the heated cotton and ridges of his muscles glided under her hands. She wrapped them around his taut middle while he encased her in the power of his arms. His palm cupped her nape, drawing her face into the crook of his neck, into the crack house of his intoxicating scent. The ecstasy of it had her fingers gripping the cliffs of his lower lats and her lids fluttering.

"If I didn't think we could do this, I'd have carried you, kicking and screaming to extraction."

"I know we can," she whispered. "I just worry what it'll cost. Risking my life is one thing. Risking yours—"

One second, she stared at the smooth contours of skin over the edge of his traps, admired the fine golden hairs on his nape. The next, his gaze burned her a second before his open mouth collided with hers. Wet silk glided over her lips in steady pressure. He swallowed her gasp and morphed it into a rumble. It vibrated the muscle under her hands.

His palm snaked up her neck and grabbed the base of her braid. With a steady tug, Piper's head gave over in a backward lull. Every ounce of preservation fled. Desire replaced fear. Curiosity replaced concern. Her shoulders sighed her relief, lazing with abandon.

Ryan supported her in his sure grip and laved at her mouth with eager pulls. His tongue teased the corner of her thin lips. More than almost anything, she wanted him inside her in every way. But she didn't dare move. Didn't care to move. Contrary to every sexual experience of her life, Piper let a man lead. And screw it all, with him kissing like he did, she'd follow him just about anywhere.

"Give me your tongue, Piper."

"What?"

She tried to meet his gaze, but with her neck exposed and his grip on her hair she could only see a semi-circle of devastating blue eyes.

"If you want me to release you, all you have to say is bronce."

Piper clamped her lips together, forbidding the word to escape.

"Good." His tongue lapped at her top lip. "Now, give me your tongue."

The organ inside her mouth toyed with her teeth, willing her mouth to open. Still her lips remained sealed. *Why did he want her tongue? If she poked out her tongue, wouldn't she look like a grade-school idiot?*

Ryan placed a sweet kiss on her chin and stepped back. Just like that, the spell shattered into a million pieces and rained on her head. The high of letting go snapped back like a gigantic rubber band. And that bitch stung. His face set in neutral. Not happy. Not sad. Not callous. Just even.

"You got out of your head for a moment. That's more than I ever expected." The idea of a smile swept over his face, tugging at his lips. Too quickly it fled. "Don't worry about me. Do. Not. You worry about detonating the garage and porch, and not getting shot. Let's get to work."

Chapter Twelve

It took all day to set the ambush. Yet, it had taken nearly no words at all. He counted two during his world famous enchiladas. And her, "Thank you," had been perfunctory. Nothing special. No wonder he couldn't find a woman to please him in and out of the bedroom. What he found attractive out of the bedroom—strong will and bravery—contradicted, and therefore precluded, his desires inside.

Despite that thought, there had been a moment that morning when Piper had become lighter than air in his arms. When she loosened her death grip on ultimate control and gave over to pleasure. Pitiful though it may be, it was the sweetest gift he'd ever received.

Ryan knocked on her bedroom door, not waiting for her to come to him. It would never really happen anyway. When she opened the door he had to clear his throat to speak.

"Just want to make sure you have the first aid kit."

Piper had scrubbed off the layers of dust that powdered their bodies like human beignets. Her ultra long hair sat atop her head, hidden by the tallest towel turban he'd ever seen. Thankfully more than terrycloth covered her middle. Though, the T-shirt and boxers weren't much better coverage.

Especially without a bra. He focused on the fresh gauze covering her wrist and not her tiny, pebbled peaks.

"I took care of it already," she said, "I didn't want you..."

When he held a palm up she trailed off. "I get it. You didn't want me touching you. You can take care of yourself. You don't need me or anyone else to help." Yep, he got that loud and clear. Ryan touched two fingers to his gritty brow before turning to go.

"That's not what I meant."

"Good night, Piper. I'll see you in a few hours."

What was it about this woman that turned him into a flat-out ass? He'd never pushed a woman to tears. Never spoken his mind. He smiled and did as told. At work and at home. The only place he let his dominance rein was on a mission or in a club.

Why?

Ryan rubbed the ache at his chest, ducked in the hallway bathroom, and closed the door. He propped his M4 next to the shower stall, put the satphone on the sink, turned the spray on as hot and as high as it would go, and then stripped. Stepping under the spray, hope bubbled. Maybe the water would boil away his thoughts. Too bad his brain didn't shut down. Sleep didn't quiet the constant hum. No chance a shower would.

Why?

He could blame his parents like any good kid would. His mother's crying was the equivalent to drowning puppies. Atrocious and heart rending. His father's absentee parenting and over the moon expectations for his only son sucked a big one. But.

Piper was right. Guilt ate him from the center of his heart to the tips of his toes.

For so long he'd been a walking, talking, smiling corpse. Because nobody saw through the looks he inherited from his mother and the charm he learned from his father. Was it penance for his sins? He hadn't wanted anyone to see his pain. Didn't want anyone to pity him. Couldn't stand letting anyone down. Not when he was the only thing his mother lived for.

The thick lather, vicious scrubbing, and beating flow weren't enough to swindle the guilt from his conscience. Still, acknowledging it eased the razor's edge. He rinsed the suds from his body and set his face beneath the spray. The phone chirped. Ryan scrambled out of the shower, dripping water all over the world, trying to reach it before the second ring.

"Noble," he answered.

"Her story checks out. Clean record and exemplary credentials from the L.A.P.D. Her older sister has a wrap sheet just as long as Piper's accolades. Mostly minor stuff, until the last few years. She has known links to the Sinaloa Federation's faction in the US." Tucker huffed. "I hate to say it, but maybe Piper got in over her head with them too. You're a hell of a convenient way out of that hell hole."

Ryan considered it for a fraction of a second. "No. She's not telling me something, but there's no way she'd work for them."

"Don't underestimate the influence of an older sibling. They're role-models. Positive or negative."

"My instinct says no."

"You mean your dick says no."

"Damn it." Ryan hoped he swung the mouthpiece up in time that Tucker didn't catch it, but the man caught everything.

"Look, you've always been a good operative. But today you became great." Well, that shocked his irritation mute. Tucker continued, "You were an instructions man. Whatever I told you, you did. No questions. No fault. If anyone changed the op, it wasn't you. That kind of fortitude is treasured beyond all others in most military outfits. But I like my men to listen to those instincts when they scream louder than me. Copy?"

"Yes, sir."

"Just make sure it's instinct doing the screaming and not your Johnson."

"Yes, sir."

The line went dead. Ryan set the phone on the counter and stared at it, and then his dick, and then his face in the foggy mirror. Pretty sure he knew who was running the show, he dried, stuffed his junk in another stolen pair of boxers, proving it wasn't calling the shots. He shoved his feet into his dust-dipped boots—because come on, who wants to walk barefoot where a pile-o-bodies had lain a few hours ago—and grabbed the phone, ruck, and his rifle. He stepped into the hallway and stopped as abruptly as if he'd smacked into a tree.

On a towel in the middle of the corridor, Piper perched on her heels. Her hands gripped the tops of her bare thighs. Eyes cast to the floor and hair neatly braided, only the slope of her forehead and bridge of her nose were visible. The rest of her body postured in perfect display. Her form coursed with lean muscles, a sculpted work of art.

Ryan's nostrils flared. The grip on his weapon doubled. His eyes didn't narrow on the usual spots. Though his cock stood at attention for her dusky areolae and beaded nipples. It bulged in utter appreciation for the neat patch of curls at the junction of her thighs. Yet, his heart ratcheted to erratic beats at the feminine curve of her waist and the bend at her hips.

Instinct and his cock joined forces.

The posture wasn't submissive, but the gesture enticed the quiet Dom inside him. Ryan dropped heels on that side of himself, straining the reins of his composure. He absorbed the sight of her. Hope flickered that when he closed his eyes her image would be seared into his vision like a vibrant sunspot. Because he didn't, for more than a few seconds, believe she would go through with this little experiment.

He'd wager a truckload of money that the first instruction he gave, no matter how sedate, would send the swell of her well-toned ass running. Which was enough to make him misty-eyed. A body like hers deserved to be pleasured. Restrained and set free at the same time. Mastered.

Her chest rose and fell in rapid succession. Buds no bigger than under-ripe blueberries pointed at him, calling him out for being a coward. Here she was, making herself vulnerable. His gaze dropped to her white knuckles, which clung for dear life to her thighs.

"Palms up. Backs of your hands resting on your thighs."

His voice sounded gruff. Like he'd gone through puberty a second time and his voice deepened yet again.

Piper's fingers slid from her skin. She raised them into the air, then turned them. With the delicacy of butterflies' wings, she rested them on her quads. Pride swelled his chest while lust did magical things to his penis. One step at a time, he neared. To her credit she stayed balanced like a proud lioness at the top of a cliff.

Ryan leaned the gun inside the bedroom, set the phone on a dresser, and the ruck on the floor. He circled around her back and awed at the definition of muscle beneath her olive skin. They V'd and X'd this way and that. Most men liked stick figures or swollen curves. He liked women fit for the furor of his appetite. The pads of her toes peeked out under the rounds of her butt and he couldn't help but lick his lips.

"Relax, Piper. You're giving yourself over to pleasure. Releasing your stranglehold on control. Giving it freely to experience the thrill of the unknown. Give yourself over to the possibility of ecstasy," he coaxed.

Her shoulders dropped. The backs of her hands sank against the tawny skin of her legs. Consequently, a blush rose on her nipples and crept up her chest.

"Beautiful. Now, stand." When she rose he stood in front of her and tipped her chin with his index finger. "While we are engaged in this scene your eyes are to stay on mine at all times." He smiled. "Unless I tell you otherwise or I am exploring parts unseen."

"Scene?" Her copper eyes flared. Her skinny red lips drew his attention. When he raised his gaze, hers remained fixed on him.

"Yes. You're not in the life, as they say. Encounters or scenes should always be negotiated prior to beginning, especially with a new partner. Hard limits should be set for safety's sake."

"Negotiated?" Both her brows raised. "This isn't a hostage situation."

"It could be."

Her breath caught in her open mouth. Ryan closed the inches between them and sealed his lips over hers. Piper's head relaxed back while his tongue delved inside her mouth. Spearmint toothpaste and her hot tongue invited him deeper. He toyed with her mouth, exploring and learning his way around. All the while her tiger eyes remained fixed to his. When she swayed he eased from her heady taste.

"Tell me your hard limits, Piper."

"I..." Her gaze flitted about the hallway. Looking everywhere. Seeing nothing.

"Eyes on me," he growled.

She found him again and her cheeks flushed.

"Piper, it's about trust. An exchange. We both give and both receive. I need to know if anything is over the bounds for you." He leaned closer, touching her cheek to his and whispering in her ear. "Can I eat your pussy? Can I tie you? Are you overly sensitive anywhere? Do you have triggers? Can I slide my dick inside your sweet cunt? Your lush ass?"

She whimpered.

"I was tested clean a year ago and haven't had any partners since. Are you on birth control?" he asked.

"How romantic," she squeaked.

"It's responsible. And Piper, when I'm inside you, there will be no pulling out. No turning back. So, if you don't want this tell me now."

"I was clean six months ago. No one since. I took a Depo shot before I left the States."

"Hard limits?" he demanded.

"Apparently none with you."

"Any experience in the world of kink, Piper?"

"Some role play once, and anal play occasionally. But I've never had...anal sex."

"And did you enjoy yourself?"

"Yes."

"At any point, if you wish to stop, what do you say?"

"Bronce." True to character her voice didn't quaver in the least. Piper Vega, always in control. Until now.

"If you want something harder, softer, longer, faster. You tell me. Do as I say, and I'll oblige you as long as I'm breathing. Do you understand?"

"Yes," she sighed.

Ryan's every muscle shook with the need to take her. Right there. Standing in the hallway. Banking the insane urge with some deep breathing, he hooked his arm behind her knee, supported her back in his other, and scooped her against his chest. She caught her bottom lip between her teeth. He strode into the bedroom and sat her on the edge of the bed.

"Lie face up. Feet toward the headboard."

With a few scoots she did as he asked, stretching her gorgeous body before him. He stepped to the low-slung foot of the bed. The end of her braid lay in an S above her shoulder, its end wrapped with a strip of tattered cloth. Pinching it between two fingers, he laid the long twine straight, pointing up from her head. He slipped the tie from her hair then one by one unwound the plaits. The closer he came to her head the longer the silky group of strands ran over his finger. Three distinct sections lay fanned over the end of the bed.

When he pulled the last of the twines from her scalp a moan parted her lips. Her eyes fluttered like they longed to close against the bliss. But their gazes remained fixed. Ryan sank his finger into the strands at the base of her skull. He lifted her head off the thin covers and circled his fingers against her scalp. Her back arched off the bed. The peaks of her breasts begged for contact. The rectangular and plentiful plateaus of her abdomen contracted.

He kissed the center of her forehead then trailed them to each temple in turn. All the while his fingers kept working. He skimmed her nose with his lips. His mouth hung over hers. She whimpered and raised her lips for his. They only whispered over her eager crimson skin, giving barely a hint of what was to come.

Ryan removed one hand from her hair, but kept her busy with the other, letting it roam about her crown. Eyes fixed on hers, with his free hand he tweaked her nipple. Her mouth fell open on a gasp. He licked his right thumb then rubbed the pad over her lower lip. Dew from her hot breath gathered on his finger, forcing him to gulp his escalating need.

Grabbing both her hands, he spread her arms wide. His weight bore palm to palm, pinning her to the mattress. He breathed over her mouth for several seconds, and then moved on without a touch. She voiced her indignation in a huff, which Ryan cut off. His lips sealed over her left nipple and he sucked the miniature raspberry-sized treat into his mouth. Her huff contorted into an airy keen. The point of his tongue lashed over her delicious peak.

A sheen of sweat broke over his body. Without a word, Ryan straightened then retrieved the roll of gauze from the first aid kit on the nightstand. Her gaze followed, but not out of obedience. The whites of her eyes were too prominent. As was the unconscious gape of her pretty mouth.

"Your hand," he demanded with his own extended toward her injured one.

Head resting on the bed and her golden-fire hair strewn about, she offered her hand palm-up without hesitation. Ryan held the end of the gauze in the center and looped the two-inch wide strip twice. He closed her fingers into a fist, sat it on the cover then looped and knotted the other end to the wooden leg of the bed. With his teeth he tore the cotton, then repeated the ritual on her other hand.

He set the roll on Piper's torso, an inch below her bellybutton. Dragging the spool along her skin, he stopped just before her tuft-covered mons. Ryan stepped back and gawked at the beauty of her surrender. His hand rubbed over the stubble covering his chin.

"The most exquisite thing I've ever seen. Whatever happens, don't move your hands."

"You know I can break these things without trying or just let go."

"Yes. I also know you won't."

"You do?"

"Yes."

"How?"

"Because I don't want you to and you don't want to disappoint me or yourself."

She nodded.

Ryan's blood surged with one-hundred-proof, lust-fueled adrenaline. It pounded through his veins. Made his back bow. The thought of slipping inside her slick channel spurred him on. He stepped out of his loose boots and shucked the boxers. Piper's legs danced in an impatient shuffle, chafing together, making the roll of white shimmy on her hips.

"Patience," he warned.

The bed dipped under his weight. He knelt beside her waist. His fingers danced up the inside of her thigh. Skin smooth as a flower petal. He neared her already-glistening sex. Piper's lungs expanded on an extended inhale, waiting. She'd have to wait some more. He skipped over her clit and plucked the gauze from her pelvis. Using his teeth, he ripped three two-and-a-half foot strips and laid two across her belly.

He looped the third length behind her neck. Her respiration kicked up a notch. As though she were running a series of sprints, the breaths came quick and steady. Ryan maneuvered the fabric beneath her head then kissed the upper curve of her mouth.

"Close your eyes."

Those thin lips spread in surprise. Her gaze remained welded with his for several seconds. The thrum in her pulse and the pant of her lungs told him the gesture wasn't defiant. That all-controlling natural set of her jaw hadn't stiffened her features since the afternoon. Still, something held her back. Not fear. She was with him all the way. But her fawn like gaze refused to sever their connection.

Ryan's grip on the gauze nearly faltered. He found himself reluctant to break that small bond as well. Her lids slid closed, fanning her cheeks with thick brown lashes. Desire vised his chest and he forgot about everything but making her his. He tied a bow at her temple then leaned his mouth to her lobe.

"Don't focus on my touch. Focus on the sensations it brings. On how they excite you. On how they push or pull you."

Easing back, he grabbed a length of wispy cotton from her belly. Ryan dragged the lighter-than-feather touch down the inside of Piper's thigh, across her calf, then over the instep of her arched foot. He looped the strip beneath her heel. With measured strokes, he worked the material up her leg to mid-thigh. Taking each end in his grip, he tied the gauze taut around her toned muscle.

A throaty moan heated the room ten degrees and forced a rumble inside his windpipe. Lust rushed his fingers to repeat the ritual on the other side. When at last he finished, Ryan finally took in his prize from head to toe and everywhere in-between. Neither rail thin nor curvaceous, Piper's capable physique rivaled that of the elite warriors in his narrow field. But the restraints and blindfold, the ruddiness of her erect nipples and swollen lips of her sex surpassed his wildest fantasies.

Unable to hold back a moment longer, Ryan grabbed the gauze at her thighs and wrenched them wide. Pink lips slicked with yearning convulsed before his eyes. Begging him. Luring him. He lowered his head to her pussy and inhaled, filling his lungs with spice.

"Good fucking God, Piper."

He gnashed at the meaty flesh of her inner thigh. His teeth clamped down mere inches from her peeking clit. The pad of his middle finger swiped at the cream glazing her slit, cutting off her sharp cry. He raised his hand to her mouth and smeared her arousal across her upper lip. Releasing his hold, Ryan crawled up her body.

"Smell your need." He bit gently at her breast. Her chest expanded on a gasp. "Does it fuck with your head like it does mine?"

"Yes," she moaned and shook her head side to side.

Ryan caught his moving target, licking the glaze from her lip and smothering her with a kiss. When his chest burned for air he left her mouth and crammed his shoulders between her spread legs. A wide strip of kinky hair covered the crest of her mons, but the rest of her delectable femininity stared him in the face. Bare as his palm and a million times more enticing.

He made a peace sign—even though he wouldn't call a truce unless she used her safe-word—and eased it along either side of her tented clitoris. His lips sealed around the soft nub a second before he tried to suck it into the back of his throat. Piper's hips shimmied, trying to escape the all-out assault. But he would not let her free, suckling a minute more before easing suction. He lashed the engorged bundle of nerves with his tongue.

"Oh shit, you have to stop. I can't come already. Ryan." A sob choked her words and garbled his name. "Ryan. Oh, fuck. Fuck. Fuck."

To keep her from knocking him out with her pelvic bone, he draped his free arm across her hips. With force, he pinned her to the bed and continued alternating the sucking and lashing. Saliva pooled on his tongue. When he swallowed the taste of Piper's aphrodisiac it punched him in the gut. If that weren't enough, the sound of her free-fall sliced him open in the sweetest way. Like a big fucking piece of cake.

"Ryan. Fuck me," she sobbed again and again. Until every tensed muscle in her body sagged as though she'd lost consciousness.

He kissed his way up her belly, and then slid the wet gauze from her face. "Open your eyes, Piper. Tell me why you're crying."

Tears clotted her lashes. Her heart thrummed beneath his own racing heart. Ryan wiped the moisture from her cheek and smoothed her hair. After a long minute of shared silence, she hiccupped.

"I don't know why I'm crying. I never cry. I..." Piper licked her lips and sniffed. "I never lose control. It's terrifying...and...intense."

"Now, tell me why you couldn't come already." While she prepared her answer he massaged her bound arms, starting with her shoulders and working to her forearms.

"I'm a one-shot girl," she moaned. "One and done. Terribly cursed, like men." A precious crinkle formed between her eyes. "Why are you smiling? It's disappointing, if not downright depressing."

"Your nipples are beaded harder than the lead tip of a bullet and your greedy cunt is creating a vacuum in this room. I believe you've always been a one-shot girl, but I'm more than up for the challenge of disproving your theory."

Chapter Thirteen

Piper had always been in control. Even if she let the man take the lead, she'd run an inner monologue of demands, hoping he'd magically key into them. ESP would have worked for her. Until Ryan.

Shock. And. Awe.

He must have excelled in the military training because he employed the tactics with dumbfounding precision. Time and again he struck her inner thoughts silent. Numbed her mind with the most intense pleasure she'd ever experienced. And promised more.

Before the final words escaped his smirking lips, he lunged for her tiny breasts. His supple mouth sealed over her sensitive areola. He tried to drink it down, like he had on her still-throbbing clit, battering the electrified bud with his relentless tongue. Without warning, Piper's back bowed at the indulgence. The gauze encircling her palms grew tighter still. Her grip threatened to crush the cotton back to its pre-processed form. The tiny fibers were the only thing keeping her from flying off the bed.

Well, that and the sun-surface-hot torso anchoring her lower half. Maybe she should have kept her mouth shut. Because just one look at his body and a second orgasm threatened to pull her under and never let go. She longed to rove the chiseled valleys of his chest with her tongue. To scout the contours of his hard back with her fingers. To cram his cock so deep inside herself she'd taste his come on her lips.

Despite all her longing, Piper surrendered to his will and had never felt so damn powerful and erotic. Ryan shifted to her other breast, but his gaze never left hers. Though transfixed on his light blues, other senses and peripheral vision catalogued everything. The tickle of his right hand skimming her belly, riding the ridge of her hip bone, then driving from her clitoris along her slit. She gave herself over to his touch. Her legs stretched wider, welcoming him inside.

But his cream-laden finger slid below her labium. The slick pad smoothed along her centerline igniting a firestorm so hot it threatened to consume her. Torrid heat bloomed in a sheen of sweat over her skin. Call him an arsonist. Ryan's traveling finger stoked the flames coursing her sex and baking her from the inside. He kneaded her perineum with sure strokes before sliding lower still.

He spiraled toward her anus and the anticipation was too much to bear. She panted like a whore in heat. Soft mews fleeing her throat the closer he came. Finally she wasn't alone in the sex-crazed chorus. His mouth broke free from her breast and he groaned. Growled, really.

"I actually ache to get inside you, Piper. If you keep making those noises, I won't be able to hold back any longer."

A laugh rode on her rushing exhale. "You're holding back?"

In answer his wet pad centered on her pulsing rosette and pushed inside to the first knuckle. A feeling in contrast to any she'd experienced before swept over her body like a wild fire. The hint of pain quickly receded to the tidal wave of pleasure. Even the bonds ratcheted the level of her excitement. Though she could break them. Though the gauze at her thighs allowed her free movement. The pressure and security made her wetter than she'd ever been.

Divide and conquer. Ryan was almost too adept at battle technique. His mouth worked her breast while his finger danced inside her ass. It wiggled, coaxing every nerve ending to life. It thrust deeper, shoving her precariously close to the edge of another orgasm. It undulated, coaxing fresh cream from her pussy.

Her head arched of its own volition, breaking their eye contact. Before she could gather the tumult into a cohesive release, Ryan's prying heat and reassuring weight left her body. Quicker than lightning, her gaze found his. But no matter how she tried she couldn't keep it locked on his.

He knelt between her spread thighs, his heavy erection filling his palm. Good gawd. If he tried to make a fist his fingers would barely meet along his ample length. Pre-cum dewed the beautiful slit along his bulbous head. Piper licked her lips, the desire to have him in her mouth and crammed down the back of her throat warring with the need to have him in her cunt.

Ryan stroked his length, the muscles across his body tensing at the pleasure. His already glistening finger, the one that had been inside her, spread his lubricant across the silk of his crown. He levered forward, brushing the tops of his thighs against her bottom. The course blond hairs covering his legs tickled. And revved her higher.

"I should swat your ass for breaking eye contact. But I can't look away from this either. And you're not quite ready for spanking. Watch me, Piper. Watch us own each other."

Her gaze flickered to his face, reveled in the taut lines of his jaw and the lushness of his lips, but he was right. She couldn't keep her eyes from their union. Ryan hefted the globes of her butt, wedging her at his hips. He levered over her and as sure as a heat-seeking missile, his wide dick found her entrance.

His width separated her lips. She bloomed for him, opening to take him all. He stuffed her entrance so full, Piper thought she'd scream in pain and delight. His blunt head retreated and he petted her pussy with it. Their juices melded. The strokes circled her clit then eased home, shoving a full two inches into her hot channel. Another roll of his hips and the tip disappeared. It stretched her so full tears pricked her eyes.

He's not going to fit. Oh my God. He's not going to fit.

No sooner had the thought entered her mind than Ryan flicked both her nipples like he tried to make a goal with a paper football. They stung and her mouth fell open with indignation, but he didn't see. Instead he crowded over her, laving each tip with gentle laps. He blew and the sensation changed. The fiery edge of her orgasm livened. Her hips undulated against his cock, urging him on with her need to be possessed.

Ryan pinched her left nipple, holding it between his roughened fingers while he held her hip with his other hand and thrust. The motion dipped her into the mattress. With a rounded holler and wiggle of her ass, Ryan stuffed her full to overflowing. His balls brushed her ass and his waist cuddled her hypersensitive nub. But she didn't see any of it. Her eyes closed against the magnitude of their coupling.

A bead of sweat dropped onto her cheek a moment before Ryan's forehead met hers. They panted together and sweated through the intensity for a long minute. When it became bearable Piper opened her eyes and found him staring back. His arms nestled beneath her shoulder blades as he gathered her close. Chest to chest they lay, his weight supported on his elbows. With their gazes fused, Ryan rocked his hips, rubbing the thick column of his dick against her swollen tissues.

"Give me your tongue."

Unlike the previous time, Piper poked her tongue into the air in offering. His lips closed over it and pumped. She fucked his mouth while he fucked her pussy. The sensations were too much to handle. Using her heels as leverage, she undulated with him.

Ryan pulled from her body then thrust to the root. They devoured each other's mouths as the tempo rose. His hard chest pressed against her tender nipples. His sack slapped her livened rosette. The thatch of hair surrounding his big cock abraded her clit. It was all too much.

Piper screamed her release into his mouth, but Ryan didn't falter. He kept pounding, cramming her full. She moaned and keened at the electricity that scorched her every nerve ending then regrouped in her core. Growing. Building again.

He broke the kiss and reached around with his right hand. That familiar finger gathered their moisture, sliding fiendishly around the lips of her sex. Like before his pad moved south, but there was no slow wind up. He found her center and pierced deep.

"Oh fuck. Ryan. Oh. Ryan."

One restraint gave way as she braced against the onslaught of titillation. Her hand rushed to his back and she clamped onto his firm lat for dear life.

"That's it, Piper. Feel me all over you. Inside you. Everywhere," he panted. "You'll come for me again before I explode."

"Yes. Yes! I'm already there. Ryan."

The fire exploded into a raging ball, the concussive force nearly knocking her unconscious. Light tunneled into a dim circle where only Ryan existed. His knowing eyes. His lust. His roar. Her world expanded in a ripple of awareness as he came, steaming her from the inside with hot spurts. The impossible width of him expanded her cunt, pulsating while he hammered one last time.

As she wished, he nested so deep she'd swear he was in her throat. His hand entwined in her hair and he held her still. Every muscle in his body strained. The sinew of pure masculinity stretched his skin. Veins bulged in his neck. Reverberation from her detonation shook her. He screamed. They screamed.

Then there were only heaves of breath and frantic heartbeats. And his clear blue gaze on her bronze.

Chapter Fourteen

Ryan woke with a jerk. For once it wasn't to a nightmare, but a reality so hot it melted his most carnal dreams to insignificant puddles. Piper's hair splayed across his chest. The curve of her naked hip nestled his growing erection. Her sweet even breaths tickled his neck. A smile played over his lips. Then, just as quickly, fell.

He hadn't planned on sleeping. He hadn't set an alarm. The room lay in shadow and his gaze flew to the bedside lamp. She must have turned it off sometime during his sex-induced coma. The phrase "sitting ducks" had never been more apt than for their current situation. If the Sinaloa found them lounged back on a pile of rumpled sheets, all he had was his dick to protect them. And the thing had proven to get him into more trouble than anything else.

"Piper. Get up." He sat and brought her up with him. Piper started, her arms flailing wildly. "It's me. It's Ryan. You're safe. But we have to move." His arms banded around her, holding tight until she caught up with his words.

"Shit," she whispered.

Depressing the button on the side of his watch, he found the time markers illuminated to muted green while the baby-blue hand and twelve-marker showed him the time.

"It's 0130."

"Ryan, I'm sorry."

"I'm not. Let's just not get dead because we got blown away."

"Blown away?"

"To heaven and back," he said.

Untangling their limbs, he stood beside the bed and took her head in his hands. The thrum of her pulse increased under his thumb. In the little bit he could make out in the darkness, the whites of her eyes shown wide and bright.

"Get dressed. Meet me downstairs. Don't turn on the light. And bring the AK with you," he ordered, without raising his voice.

She nodded her compliance. He smashed a kiss to her warm lips then shoved his feet in boots, stuffed the phone into the ruck, grabbed it and the M4, and bolted. As he always did when heading into the unknown, Ryan dowsed his nerves in ice water. Training was an amazing tool. Do something long enough and it becomes automatic. So, he didn't allow himself time to worry about all the things that could go wrong. He stopped at the top of the stairs, closed his eyes, and strained his hearing. In the distance coyotes yipped and howled. At the window a bug beat itself against the glass in a relentless effort to reach the bright light of the hallway.

Never go toward the light, buddy.

Other than the breathing of the house and the stir of wildlife, nothing moved below that caused him pause. When things got too still, too quiet, then he'd worry. With his swinging junk, Ryan took the stairs three at a time, rounded the corner, and shot to the window. On the dark horizon nothing moved. He wished he'd gotten the thermal imagery unit back from Piper the first night, but he hadn't wanted to set himself in temptation's path.

Ryan tied off the boots, shoved his feet into his fatigues, pulled on socks, and secured the boots to his feet. He dragged the PIG pack over his head then turned toward Piper. Two more steps and she appeared at the top landing. When she descended, her gaze darted around the room, and then teetered between the windows. Her hand crushed the strap of the AK-47 hanging over her shoulder.

"All clear for now." He secured the Velcro straps around his torso.

"We're late. We can't screw this up because we were fucking. Here's your night vision."

They'd planned to be in position by midnight, knowing the deliveries always arrived between 0200 and 0300. So, yeah, they were late, but not too late.

"I'd like to think we did a little more than just fuck, but stay alive and we'll talk about it later." Ryan took the monocular she offered and dropped to his knees before her. He pulled the band over his head, letting them hang loose around his neck. Next he unzipped his pack and held out a detonator. A single strip of electrical tape crossed the back of the remote. "For the garage."

"I'll blow it as soon as their rear wheels disappear."

"As soon as. The bodies probably stink like a three-day-old battlefield. We can't risk them getting clued in and backing out or warning the others."

"I've got it," she snapped. Her feet tap-danced on the terracotta tiles.

When she reached for the device he tried to grab her hand, but she pulled out of range.

"I need the other detonator." Her eyes narrowed and she settled him with a glare.

A big ole *what the fuck* reared its head in Ryan's mind. Of course, they didn't have time to explore it. The look on her face said she didn't want to anyway. Maybe ever. What the hell had he done to elicit such a reaction? Only minutes ago she snuggled him like he were the only source of heat in Alaska. Here in the winter, after the sun set, temperatures dropped to the forties. Perhaps she'd only been cold. As cold as his insides felt at her unaffected manner.

From the pack he pulled the black remote with two tape strips crossing its back. "Give me your hand."

"We don't have time for this."

"Then I suggest you give me your hand."

Piper snapped out her palm. Had he been three inches closer, she'd have smacked him backward. Ryan placed his hand beneath and it spread an inch on every side, dwarfing hers.

"Whatever it is. You can tell me. I'll help you any and every way I can." At her feet he begged. For damn near half a minute he waited, despite the voice in his head telling him to move his ass and get in position. She didn't budge, soften, or even seem to breath. "If you refuse to let me in—if you take off on your own agenda—I'll hold you accountable for the death of innocents."

"No more than I'll hold myself. Let's get in position."

Despite the anger boiling his blood, Ryan kissed her palm before placing the remote over the show of affection. To his delight, her lower lip quivered. Just one little shake before she clamped it between her teeth. He pulled out the third and final remote detonator and slid it into a snap pocket on the front of his pack. Standing, he slung the ruck over his back along with his M4.

"In positions," he agreed.

They hustled through the house and across the back porch. Thick clouds huddled overhead, adding a layer of doom to the already heavy night. Ryan headed left to the southwest corner of the jail, while Piper turned right to take cover at the northwest edge of the house. He didn't look back, despite the gut-twisting need. Pulling up the thermal imagery monocular, he scanned the rise of the foothills. The caravan would come over the rise and down a mile stretch to the front of the property. He just hoped everything went according to plan. Two against twenty-two weren't great odds.

Chapter Fifteen

When he didn't look back Piper sighed with relief. Had he turned to check on her or blow her a goodbye kiss, he'd have noticed the bulges at the back of her shirt. Then she'd have had to explain why she'd taken two handguns and two extra magazines off the dead bodies yesterday. Around the side of the house, she broke into a dead sprint all the way to the front.

At the main entrance, she bolted through the lit archway. Heart in her throat and her stomach dragging two feet behind, she pulled metal charges from molded balls of C-4. She cleared the archway then moved to the interior of the house, pulling every charge on the front half of the house. Piper didn't let the sting of guilt inside, though it rapped hard on her chest. Her deception couldn't be helped. She had a mission to complete too. It ran hand in hand with Ryan's, save for one exception.

Émile Gabrone must not die in this battle.

What sounded like a hail of bullets crashed against the front windows. Piper dove behind the chair Ryan had used as a bed the first night and curled into a ball. Falling glass didn't follow the cutting noise. She peeked from behind the furniture. Rain drops the size of gumballs pelted the glass in waves. She swallowed the sickness rising from her belly and stood.

Great, I'm going to freeze to death before this thing even gets started.

Hopeful, if not confident, the house wouldn't come crumbling down around Gabrone's ears, Piper steeled herself for the onslaught of rain and frigid temperatures. She sprinted for the position she should have posted for the last twenty minutes. Rounding the archway into the blasting downpour, she skidded into the solid wall of Ryan's chest. His hands clamped her upper arms and shoved her back beneath the eve. Water dripped from her forehead. Trickled down her nose. But it ran in torrents down his neck and face and poured from his narrowed brows.

"What were you doing, Piper?" His voice held none of the affection she'd grown to expect in such a short time. Its deep growl meant to intimidate, not entice as it had before.

"I..." Words altogether failed her.

"The truth," he demanded with a small shake.

"I needed a jacket," she whispered. It hurt to look him in the eye and lie. But she had to keep his gaze from wandering. "I didn't want to die of hypothermia before they got here." Then, with more gusto, she turned the tables. "What are you doing?"

Ryan's right hand left her arm and reached behind him. He pulled a small square from his ruck then handed it to her. "It's not much, but it'll keep the water off of you."

Her heart squeezed. She accepted the digitally-patterned rubber he shook out into an actual poncho. "What about you? You're soaked through already."

"I've lived through worse. Put it on and let's move. And don't scare me like that again. When I rounded the corner and you weren't in position I lost a good two years."

After pulling the poncho over her head and grabbing her AK from Ryan, Piper stepped so he faced the rain and the muddled mountain scenery. She stretched onto tiptoe, melding her lips to his. "I'm sorry," she said. And she was. Sorry for lying. Sorry for not confiding in him. Sorry for the possibilities that would never be between them.

He walked her to her corner position, then released her hand and moved like a panther across the lawn. Fast. Sleek. Silent. She lost sight of him only a few yards away in the curtain of rain that distorted the light from the house. Sidling close to the structure, she managed to stay mostly dry. She waited several minutes then dug two pairs of handcuffs from the base of a shrub she'd buried them near the day before. The cool metal chilled her skin as she tucked them into the back pocket of her dark jeans.

Not ten minutes after Ryan escaped her sight, his sharp warning whistle split the air. Though muffled in the deluge the tone jolted her heartbeat into overdrive. A cold sweat broke out across her entire body. She longed to run to the front corner of the house and watch them come over the rise, but he'd warned her against it. The house-front's decorative lighting would give her away with a stray glance.

Piper rested her forehead against the stucco, breathed through her nose then out her mouth. She counted all the while, keeping estimated mental tabs on the caravan's progress. Vomit reflex under control, she turned toward the garage, detonator in one hand and AK in the other. The garage door rumbled open and everything went quiet. The rain faded into the background. In her ear, the pound of her heartbeat waned.

Nothing mattered in that moment, except the rumble of the engine as the blacked-out Escalade rolled into view. The wiper blades slashed on the windshield in a vicious back and forth, trying and failing to keep the onslaught at bay. Tucked into shadow as Ryan planned, she didn't worry they'd see her. Especially with the cover of rain. She didn't even worry about the number of lives she was about to take. She only worried about three. Hers. Ryan's. And Matthew's.

Chapter Sixteen

Focus, Noble.

Ryan banished his inner turmoil. He knew she'd lied to him, but what the hell could he do about it now? They were about to be in the throes of a firefight. Even though it helped more than it hurt, sometimes it sucked to have eyeballs that doubled as lie detectors.

The adrenaline that rode him hard washed away like a receding tide. Quiet calm took its place. He raised the silencer on the barrel of his riffle and aimed the crosshairs of his scope on the bus driver's head. Sure, two detonations as loud as a sonic boom would rock the air, but it was still nice when the bad guys didn't hear which way the bullets were coming from. They'd see the barrel flash. Or at least the last couple would. Not that it would do them any good. He wished he had another silencer for Piper's gun, but he hoped she didn't have to use it. Pushing the button that would end a handful of people's lives was hard enough without staring your target in the eyes and pulling the trigger.

Vehicle one rolled by, headed for the garage. The faded school bus headed toward him. Its rusted wheels rolled to a stop only six yards away. Heat warmed his face and the flash of fire lit the world all around as the first bomb detonated. Ryan

squeezed the trigger. The Hispanic man, with a
tattoo of Santa Muerte staining his bulged
shoulder, slumped over the extra large steering
wheel.

Screams lit the night. All in reaction to the
blast still rattling windows. Barrel up, Ryan raced
to the northwest corner of the building. Two men in
the front seat stared, mouths open at the fireworks.
The back hatch opened. Two sets of boots hit the
ground. He ended the lives of the men in the SUV—
driver and shot-gun rider—in a smooth level of his
riffle. One bald head leaned into the front seat,
hands searching his drooping compadres. He never
found what happened to them. The impact of the
bullet sent him sprawling into the dark recesses of
the vehicle.

Side doors fanned open on either side, but
the occupants had learned their lesson. All
remained behind the cover of the black Cadillac.
Shouts were exchanged, but he didn't hear them.
They blurred into the mush of his brain as his gaze
locked on the tail car parked at the back porch. Not
as planned. They'd taken a gamble and lost. Too
many possibilities and not enough remote
detonators.

The matching SUV bloomed like a flower. Men
leaped from the interior, weapons up, looking for
the fight. Ryan ignored his constricting chest and
snipped three of the men. But that left four more
for Piper to deal with. A bullet smacked the ground
ten feet from his boot. A quick reminder he had his
own shit to handle. And fast.

The first bullet opened a floodgate and they
rained down on his head as frequently as moisture
from the cloud above. He flattened against the
building and waited. And wished. Wished Piper was
okay. Wished Piper would blow the front just to

create a diversion. When the later didn't happen he prayed to God the former did.

Twenty long seconds later the frequency ebbed. He dropped onto his back two feet into the wide open. Two sets of legs shown in the space beneath the car. One shot to a calf. Another to a foot. Ryan ended their flailing with two more bullets. The last two goons proved to be quick studies, jumping into the belly of the metal beast.

Two more hulking bodies littered the ground near the house, next to the ones he'd take out. So, she'd gotten two. She only had two left. Piper could do it.

Ryan rolled to cover. Spitting the mud that sloshed onto his mouth, he got to his feet in a flash and waited. The rain left as quickly as it had come. The sudden silence was more than he could bear. He wanted to call to Piper. He wanted to run into the open and draw their fire. But he wouldn't make those rookie mistakes. If he died, so would Piper. He'd told her about the rendezvous, but, not wanting to worry her, had left out the part about negotiating a minefield.

With silent steps he backed down the building to his original position and on to the southeast corner. Taking both ends of the building into his periphery, he held. By now they knew it was a lone shooter on their left. With two of them, no doubt they'd take the split and attack from both directions. At least, that's what he'd do.

From this vantage point he could see the end of car two, but more importantly, he could see the tail car and the trail of bodies leading to the house. None of which boasted bronze hair and a shapely ass.

He'd nearly given up hope on his quarry when a tiny scrape of rock on metal gave away the

man on his right, a split second before his barrel
peeked around the corner and sprayed. Ryan fell
back behind the jailhouse, rolled toward the other
end of the building, and took one shot. The man
didn't even stumble, just fell, his shoulder-length
brown hair pooling with blood.

Ryan maintained his point, let the M4 rest at
his side, and removed his sidearm. He went high
this time. He kept everything close and lifted on
tiptoes. With half an eye, he shot the behemoth in
the shoulder then retreated. Ryan circled around in
the opposite direction, keeping away from the
building and staying on the grass.

The screaming had quieted, but when he
stepped from behind the jail the bus erupted in
cries and high-pitched squeals. The gunman
turned, but it was too late. Ryan's bullet caught
him in the temple. With a weary eye on the bus,
Ryan advanced on the SUV. He checked the bodies.
Counted his dead seven. Counted five from the
other Escalade.

He wanted to go to her, but had to check the
bus or he could get them both killed, if he missed a
guard or impersonator among the hostages. Ryan
scanned the house, surrounding area, and the
jailhouse as he made his way toward *the cheese* as
he and his sister used to call the yellow buses.

When he stepped onboard the occupants
sucked the air out of the cylindrical tube with their
collective gasp. Most of the women cowering in the
seats were no more than eighteen. A few older. A
couple far, far too young. Keeping his pistol up,
Ryan removed his left hand and presented his
palm. He spoke in Spanish.

"I am sorry you had to witness the violence.
My name is Ryan. I will not hurt you. I am not part
of any cartel. I am here to make sure you are

reunited with your families." Some women straightened from their huddles. A few shrank deeper into the seat as he advanced one step at a time to the head of the aisle. "For your safety and mine, if anyone on this bus works for the Sinaloa or is loyal to "El Chapo" Guzmán Loera, you need to stand slowly with your hands in the air."

They became statues, the creepy pictures in haunted houses where nothing moved but the eyes. As if in choreographed unison, every gaze traveled toward the back of the bus. Every gaze except three. Two belonged to twin girls balled together on the second row on the right. The third gaze stared unblinking and fake shrinking from the back row. Yes, the woman hugged herself—which displayed thick biceps and powerful forearms. Yes, the woman's lower lip quivered. Combined with the searing hatred radiating from her eyes, it only made her false emotion more pronounced.

Ryan let his pistol drop to his side. He smiled at the ladies. Not the full-on wattage, but an *I'm sorry and everything's going to be okay* curve of the mouth. He walked casually as he talked.

"Please remain calm and in your seats. Is anyone hurt? Injured in any way?" Again no one moved. "I am trained in first aid and can help you, if you let me."

While he walked, his gaze swept one side to the next, always keeping the woman in the back in his sight. A brunette with graying temples, who sat six seats up from the faker, raised her hand.

"Sí, Señora?" Ryan bowed.

"Señor, as far as I am aware no one is hurt, but we have not eaten in many hours. Maybe an entire day now. We are thirsty too," she whispered.

"Thank you for telling me. There are supplies in the house we can use before we leave." Ryan assured her and the others, speaking loud enough for everyone to hear. He took another step toward the back. The brunette grabbed his hand, pulling him up short.

"Thank you, angel. Thank you for saving us. We are saved." She kissed the back of his hand. When she released him, she clapped and raised her hands to the heavens. Others joined in, creating a cacophony of sound in the metal enclosure. More cheers erupted for their good fortune.

All except the woman at the back.

Ryan holstered his gun, regained his lost step, took another. Two seats from the back, the woman with long black hair and a darker attitude launched toward him. The knife blade glinted in the licking flames from the burning garage. She rushed hard, aiming right for his gut. He concaved his belly and snatched her wrist. With a twist, Ryan raised her hand into the air and rotated another fifteen degrees.

"You killed my Dante." Her scream rattled his eardrum and quieted the revelry of the others.

Balled knuckles from her other hand sailed at his face. Ryan caught her fist in his palm, kicked the red latch of the rear door up, and shoved her through the gap. She landed on her butt, the knife still in her stubbornly strong grip. He jumped to the pavers, willing Piper to show herself already. It had been too long. Far too long.

"I am sorry I took someone you love, but what you're doing is not right." He pointed toward the bus. "These women...these children deserve to be with the people they love and who love them back.

"Drop the knife." He softened his voice. "We can reunite you with your family." When she balked, he added, "or give you a new start."

She rose from the ground to her full height, somewhere in the neighborhood of five-and-a-half feet. Her mouth thinned and she pointed the knife at him. "I'd rather give you an ending." Jerking her head toward the bus, she added, "I'll just give them to Los Zetas, and get my money."

The woman slid a furtive glance to the corpses littering the ground two yards behind. Her gaze widened at an MP7 skimming the tips of the nearest man's fingers. Ryan's fingers itched for his own H&K. Yet, he ignored the urge.

"Don't even try. You'll be dead before you get to it," he barked.

Her body coiled and Ryan had a fraction of a second to decide his course of action. Kill her? Don't?

He burst forward, cleared the gap, and rocketed into the air. His arm locked around her throat. They landed hard, water splashing around them. He pinned her knife hand to the stone with his other. She bucked and Ryan splayed his legs wide on either side for leverage.

Despite her pinched windpipe, his six-foot two-and-a-half inches and two-hundred-eighteen-pound frame pinning her to the ground, she crawled forward. She ditched the knife and clawed at the bricks. Her fingers skimmed the submachine gun's stock. Ryan increased his grip on her throat.

"Don't do this," he pled. But she only dug in harder, moving another inch in her efforts. Fuck, he hated killing women.

The last bit of wind wheezed from her lungs and still she fought. Her bloody fingertips curled around the butt, dragging it closer.

Piper picked that moment to step onto the porch.

Joy warred with dread inside him.

The woman's finger closed, looping the trigger. She pulled off one shot before Ryan snapped her neck.

Screams erupted from the bus, but he paid them no attention. He was running before the echo of the blast reached his ear. Piper ran too. They cleared the lawn in seconds and collided in an embrace. Reaching beneath her arms, he lifted her like a child. Her hands looped around his neck and he crushed her to him. His face buried in the lee of her jaw. He inhaled her.

Too soon she pushed back, seeking his gaze. "Are you okay?"

He nodded. "You?" She mirrored his nod. Pure joy lightened his chest and made breathing a hell of a lot easier. Reluctantly, he set her on her feet. "I need you to take this," he said, shrugging off his ruck. "Go to the kitchen and pack it with anything that'll travel—and a lot of it."

"Sure." Piper's lips brushed his cheek before she took the ruck and disappeared into the house.

Eyes scanning the yard, Ryan hopped onto the bus and distributed the cases of water stacked beneath the driver's seat. When he hoisted the dead man onto his shoulders and piled him with the others, satisfaction pillowed his conscience. The bastard had sat on water while the women he hauled to hell suffered thirst.

Piper joined them on the bus and he set her to task handing out the chips and cake snacks she scored from the house. Ryan started the engine and pulled several hundred yards away from the facility. "Okay, everyone cover your ears. One more big boom." He detonated the facility. It wasn't as big a blast as he'd have liked, but it did the trick. No one would use the place to hold people captive ever again.

Satisfied, he sat, shoved the old clunker into gear, and shoved on to the next part of their long journey.

Chapter Seventeen

Piper's hands shook like a tweeker in withdrawal. So, when a lady with kind eyes offered to pass out the goodies she obliged. She wrestled off the rain slicker, hoping breathing would come more easily. Her knees shook and she sank back, her bottom barely catching the edge of a seat. Head between her legs, Piper sucked air in rapid, shallow breaths.

She'd never killed anything bigger than a bug. Yeah, she'd been trained to, if the necessity ever arose. But her duty was to protect and serve. Yet, she'd ended three lives tonight with bullets to various vital body parts and blown seven more to pieces. She covered her face and cursed the tears welling in her eyes.

A tiny hand patted her back in easy rhythm. Another held her upper arm in comforting embrace. Little, hot fingers warmed her cool skin. Her tears stalled. She turned as the bus lurched forward. With quick arms, she steadied two young girls. Five maybe. Their dark pigtail braids tattered. Their faces streaked with evidence of their own crying. They had the same coffee-brown eyes, thin lips, and pixie noses. Twins. Other than their clothing, she couldn't tell them apart.

"Don't worry," the nearest said in quick Spanish. "The angel saved us. He will protect you too."

Piper scooted farther into the seat and followed the delicate finger pointing toward the front of the bus. "The angel?"

"Yes, him," the other girl agreed. "He'll take you to your family. Do you have a family?"

Piper nodded. If she spoke, she might burst into ugly sobs.

"My name is Alma," the nearest announced, placing a hand on her pink top. She hitched a thumb toward her sister. "That's Alisa. What's your name?"

"Piper," she croaked.

In the red top, Alisa shifted round her twin and brushed Piper's plait.

"I like your braids." Piper smiled.

They all lurched into the air as the bus hit a large dip. The girls crowded into Piper's lap and she braced them with one arm while struggling to keep their seat with the other.

"Sorry," Ryan hollered. In the reflection of the rectangular mirror, he held a satellite phone to his ear and continued barking what she could only assume were not nice words into the thing.

"It's okay, angel," Alma called back.

Ryan's mouth quirked into a smile. Dry mud cracked around his lips. Apprehension tickled Piper's nape. What was he talking about? Why was he upset? What did he know?

Alma turned toward Piper, pulling her attention away from Ryan. Her pigtails swung wide. Impossibly tiny lips pursed, then thinned. She glanced at her sister and buried her head against the little girl's shoulder.

"What is it?" Piper asked.

"What will happen to us?" Alisa answered. In unison both girls shuddered.

"What do you mean? You'll go back to your family." Piper hugged them close. Maternal instincts honed by years of taking care of her sisters kicked in.

"Our family is gone." Alma cried against Piper's chest. The girl's hot breath seeped through her shirt and straight into her heart. "Mamma left us when we were babies and the bad men...made Daddy sleep with Mary and Jesus."

Alisa hid her eyes with her small hands and shook her head, as if trying to shake the memory loose.

Any guilt Piper harbored about taking the lives of the Sinaloa fled. Anger took over. And concern. What would happen to these little girls? She didn't know the answer. If they truly had no family, she refused to let them get devoured by the system. But what could she do? Her cup overfloweth with problems to handle.

"You'll be safe. Right now, that's all I know. You will be protected." Piper squeezed the girls close and settled in for a long, bumpy ride. The girls snuggled against her chest. She eased her head onto the seat back. Her sigh was cut off mid-exhale by the halt of the bus.

Ryan cut the engine and stood.

"Did everyone get something to eat?" His gaze zeroed in on her and his brow pinched.

Piper looked down at the tiny twins both shaking their heads. *Oh Lord. Way to be motherly.* She grabbed the pack the kind woman had returned and fished out snacks for the three of them. Speaking English, she asked, "What's wrong? I thought evac was fifteen miles away."

"It was. I negotiated to five, but we have to walk it," he replied in kind.

"What?" she balked.

"Please everyone," he spoke in their native tongue. "I need your attention." When the murmurs quieted he continued. "There will be a helicopter waiting to take us to the embassy where we'll make arrangements to reconnect you with your families." Some of the ladies fidgeted. "You are not in trouble and will not be held on any past indiscretions. In order to reach the HELO we must walk awhile. Five miles. The path is not steep. But," he paused. Deep ridges bracketed his mouth in a grimace. "It's narrow. Three feet. And we are literally walking through a minefield."

Murmurs grew to a low rumble. The vanilla cake with strawberry cream filling sponged away every bit of saliva in Piper's mouth. Alisa and Alma chomped away on theirs, happy little girls.

"We'll be fine," Ryan reassured. "I've cleared the path and run it several times. All you have to do is stay in a single file and follow me."

He took two casual steps and bent on one knee in front of their seat. Hand covering his heart, he hit the girls with a smile so sweet Piper's molars ached. "I didn't know they let supermodels on this bus."

Alma squinched her nose and giggled.

"They let angels on the bus." Alisa shrugged. "Of course they let super bottles. Otherwise, we wouldn't have anything to drink."

Rich peals of laughter rumbled from Ryan's chest and did funny things to Piper's insides. "Of course," he agreed. He rustled around the backpack for a moment, then pulled out a pack of chips. "How would you ladies like to have a contest?"

Their little butts wiggled with joy, grinding tiny hipbones into her already sore legs. They bobbed their heads and flung their arms with abandon. Only her embrace of them kept the chaos controlled.

"Okay! Okay! We're going to take a little walk, but we don't want the sand to mess up your pretty shoes. So, I'm going to carry you." He pointed to Alma and the little girl fist-pumped the air. "And Piper is going to carry you." Alisa gave a seesaw of her shoulders and a wide smile.

"Now, we're going to see which of you can count the most stars. It's a cloudy night. You have to keep your eyes wide. Can you do that?"

"Yes!" they cheered.

Switching to English he added, "Piper, I need you in the back. If anyone steps out of line, holler. Three feet isn't much, but it's all we've got."

"It's not all we've got." She didn't elaborate. There wasn't time. This wasn't the place. But this man made her knees weak, her cunt tight, and her ovaries thrum. And no man got near her ovaries. Ever.

He smiled and lifted Alma into his arms. When he turned away she wondered if she'd ever get the chance to realize the possibilities with Ryan. She wondered if he'd ever forgive her deception.

Chapter Eighteen

Ryan lifted weights and trained year round. He routinely carried seventy-five pounds of weapons and survival gear on his back. He'd hauled fallen warriors over miles of uneven terrain in the worst conditions. But none of it compared to toting forty pounds of wiggling giggling child.

His biceps quivered. Tendonitis flared in his left elbow. The ache in his shoulders turned to pain a mile back. Yet, he'd never had such a deep conversation in his entire life. This girl was wicked smart and tenderhearted as they came.

When the lights of the Chinook came into view and grew bigger with each passing step, so too did his unwillingness to let her go. Orphaned by choice then by murder, she and her sister deserved a family.

He hugged Alma to him. "Ready to fly?"

"Yes," she squealed. "I counted google and two hundred fifty-one stars. Did you know google was a number? Do I win a prize?"

"Absolutely."

The chopper landed, tail loader open, stirring dust and rock with its massive duel blades. He covered Alma's eyes, stepped aside, and motioned for the women to move ahead to the ramp. Miracle of miracles, each bedraggled lady strode past with all their limbs intact.

From the bay door Sloan and Baine took up defensive positions toward the middle of the line, all-seeing eyes on the horizon. Ryan looked at Alma tucked under his chin, and then back at the married couple and their matching M4s on point. He'd get the twins a family before this day was done.

At the back of the Chinook, Khani flashed him a salute, and he returned the sentiment. She'd given them ten fewer miles to walk and would catch hell about it from Commander Tucker. He owed her big time. She ushered the women onto the chopper, doling out instructions as they passed, which is what she did best.

The nice older lady passed among the line and blew him a kiss. Most just nodded thanks. But the one they should really thank brought up the rear. If it weren't for Piper, he'd have left them to the fates. A little fact that burned a hole in the lining of his stomach.

Sweat beaded on Piper's upper lip and matted whips of her copper hair to her forehead. When her gaze lit on Alma, her eyes smiled. She met his gaze and pointed to Alisa—her twin's name, one of the many things he'd learned from Alma on the long trip—and her mouth followed suit, stretching wide. Alisa's head lay nestled under Piper's chin, much like Alma's. Only her mouth hung open in the kind of dead-to-the-world sleep reserved for the young. Alisa's arms hung limp by her side and Ryan wondered how the hell Piper carried the girl all that way. Then he remembered the curve of her hips, ample ass, and saw she'd put it to good use.

Closer and closer Piper came and the deeper and deeper her smile fell. "I don't think I can give her up," she admitted when reaching him.

"I'm not in near the hurry I thought I'd be," he agreed. "But I have an idea and some people I want you to meet."

They walked toward Sloan who turned to meet them with Baine only feet off her heels.

"Wow," she mouthed then slid him a glance. "What? Do you guys only employ hot people?"

"I could get you a job." He winked.

Sloan was a master at training her features. But he'd worked with her long enough to notice the questions flare in her amber eyes when she studied Piper. And the hitch in her breath when she really looked at the girls for the first time.

"Sloan. Baine. I'd like you to meet Piper, Alma, and Alisa." Ryan pointed to them each in turn. It warmed him to see Ms. bold and independent, Piper Vega, ease closer to his side.

"Come in town to visit old friends and we get put to work." Baine shrugged. "I like it."

The girl slept through a jarring ride down a goat path through a minefield and the deafening *whoosh* of Chinook blades. Yet, at the rumble of Baine's voice, Alisa rubbed her eyes with tiny fists and sat straight in Piper's arms. One look at Baine and her brows shot to the sky. "You're big." Her gaze moved from his head, down his body, and up again. "Furry too," she added with a giggle.

Alma joined in the laughter.

"You're small and hairless," Baine countered in smooth Spanish with a hint of his British accent. A glint of mischief sparkled in his gaze.

"Nuh-uh." Alisa shook her head. She showed her hair as evidence, exaggerating the back-and-forth.

"She's not small, because she looks like me. And I have muscles." Alma scrunched her face and presented her biceps. She grunted with effort, her balled hands shaking.

"Wow. I apologize. You're both hairy and have sturdy muscles with big potential," Baine conceded.

Both girls chortled and begged to pet his face. While he obliged them everyone shook hands, keeping a close eye on the horizon.

"You must be the willing hostage who's gotten our boy into a heap of trouble?" Sloan said, sizing Piper with a sweeping gaze, but keeping her eyes averted from the girls.

Ryan knew the girls brought back painful memories from Sloan's past. Long ago, near the same age as the twins, she'd been made an orphan. Her African mother and American father were killed before her eyes by an arms dealer's militia. Then The Devil had made her a child slave. A fate Alma and Alisa would have met, had it not been for Piper. His gaze flew to his bronze beauty. Her back straight, jaw set, she gave Sloan as good as she got. And not many people could do that.

"I am," Piper said.

"Good. It's about time the good soldier got into a little trouble." Sloan took a step closer to him and patted his arm. Gaze locked on his, she asked in English, "Where are the girls' parents?"

"Mother left when they were babies and the Sinaloa killed their father when he attacked the men taking them. According to Alma, they have no other family. All gone before they were born."

Alma leaned toward Sloan and toyed with a wisp of her dark hair. "Your hair is black and pretty like mine. Why are you hiding it under that hat?"

Sloan's honeyed gaze met with the young girl's and she covered her mouth with her hand. Lashes batted frantically as she sucked in two fortifying breaths. She pulled the black beanie from her head and placed it on Alma. "It's to keep me warm, but you can use it more than I can. And thank you. I think your hair is lovely."

Ryan hated to see his friend hurt. This hit too close to home. And, obviously hurt. In all the time they worked together, he'd only seen Sloan cry once.

Baine followed suit, crowning Alisa with his cap. In thanks, the girl threw her arms around his neck and refused to let go. He dropped the riffle to his side and looped his forearm around her bottom. "I've got her," he said to Piper. "I'm sure your arms are tired, carrying this big girl all that way."

"Thank you." Whether from the absence of Alisa or the cold, Piper wrapped her arms around her chest and shuddered.

"You're soaked through," Sloan said with a nod at him. "And Piper's not far from it. Let's get you guys into the HELO, then we'll talk."

Everyone took a step toward the aircraft except Piper. Ryan stopped and turned to face her full on. She pulled the ruck from her back and offered it to him. He stared at it as though it were a live mine.

"Thank you," Piper whispered. "Thank you for everything."

"Thank me on the chopper." He shifted Alma to his other side and grabbed her uninjured wrist.

"I'm not going." She tugged against his hold.

Ryan's entire body tightened. The cold and wet threatening to freeze his bones for the last three hours turned to steam.

"Why," he began, but stopped. His voice was sharp and too loud for tiny ears.

"Alma, why don't you come with me, Baine, and Alisa? We'll get some blankets and food, and have a picnic on the plane."

"But it's a helicopter," she corrected.

"You're right," Sloan conceded. She raised her arms and Alma leaped to her.

"Thanks," Ryan said.

Baine and Sloan huddled the girls close and hurried through the gusting wind. When they disappeared into the back of the Chinook, Ryan snapped his head around. He grabbed Piper's other arm above the wrist and loomed over her.

"Why won't you trust me, Piper?"

"Trust you? I don't even know you." Her sharp jaw canted in defiance.

"You knew me enough to give your body. But, so help me Piper, I want it all."

She blushed and shook her head. "All of what?"

"I want you. Your body. Your mind. Your trust."

"You have to earn trust," she countered.

"And haven't I? I mean, what more does a man have to do? Lay his body over a mine to prove his…" Ryan faltered. To prove his what? Love? Lust? Infatuation? Hell, he didn't know, yet. But he wanted the time to find out. "…to prove himself worthy."

"I didn't ask you to do any of this. All I wanted was for you to let me go."

"So, what? You could get yourself killed? You're one woman, Piper. Damn capable. But, still, one person without the necessary equipment and resources to do whatever the hell it is you're trying to do." He pinned her forearms to his vest with one arm, locked her nape in his other, and brought her face inches from his. "Tell me what you're trying to do."

"I'm trying to save an American citizen the Sinaloa took six months ago. His name is Matthew Reece."

Wow, a knife to the heart hurt like a bitch. He should have known—really, he'd had one to the hand and another in the side. Yet, the sting of this one threatened to grind his teeth to nubs. She risked her life to save another man. He'd known she was up to something and he'd run the gamut of hypotheses. In search of a sister. Her mother. Revenge for a fallen partner. But a man? The way she'd given herself to him so completely, he'd never allowed the possibility to enter his mind.

"And you thought they held him at that facility?" He gestured in the direction of the compound.

Her eyes widened. Not the question she'd been expecting, he guessed. She probably expected him to ask about the guy. He wanted to. Truth was, it didn't matter. If it was her dentist or her lover, he'd help because it—check that—*he, some other man,* mattered to Piper.

"No." She recovered with a couple of blinks.

"Then why, for fuck's sake, would you allow them to capture you?"

"Émile Gabrone is the book keeper. He has a laptop with lists of cargo, abduction locations, final destinations, payouts. Everything."

"That's why you locked yourself in the office."

"But the master list wasn't on the desktop. It only has current manifests."

"Say I let you go. In the middle of the damned desert with a minefield as your playground. What the hell is your next move?"

"I have to go back."

"To the compound?"

"Yes. I pulled the detonators from all the explosives at the front of the house. I couldn't chance Gabrone getting killed."

Ryan straightened and dropped her arms.

"I couldn't risk you not listening to me," she pled.

"I listen to you, Piper. Even when you don't speak. I listen to the cues your body gives me. I can tell you're scared by the squint of your brow. Anxious to get back by the shuffle of your feet. Cold by the gooseflesh on your neck. And despite it all, horny by the catch of your breath and the flush of your lips when I held you close.

"We'll do what you need to do. We'll even do it your way. You and me. I'm coming with you. And you will tell me everything."

"I can't let you—"

"You don't have a choice," he barked.

"Okay," her voice quivered.

"You've lied to me once, Piper. Don't do it again. No matter how much it hurts. We both deserve the truth and are tough enough to handle it."

"I am sorry." She swatted at a tear, and then shrugged. "I've never been a team player. Five partners in as many years on the force should tell you something."

"We all have shit to work on." Ryan held out his hand.

"Even you?"

"Especially me, but that's a story for another time. Let's get some dry clothes, food, and fresh packs. Then we'll see how Gabrone fared in the blast."

Chapter Nineteen

The girls planted wet kisses on either side of her cheeks, and then trotted down the aisle dodging feet and legs.

"It's amazing, a child's resilience." Sloan sank into the last seat in the row to her left and whispered the words as though she'd thought them and accidentally said them aloud.

"You can't let them go into the system," Piper countered.

"You're right. I can't. I just hope my husband can get on board." Sloan sighed.

Having snuck in on their tête-à-tête from the ground, Baine tugged Sloan's face to his as he knelt. "He already is, love."

Piper left the couple to their intimate moment and subsequent face sucking and watched the girls. They neared the cockpit where Ryan stood talking to Khani Slaughter. The woman scared the shit out of Piper. A task not easily accomplished. But a manner as gruff as her own combined with fire-orange lips, a full face of make-up, and rumbling gray eyes all did the trick. The twins ignored her, cutting off their heated conversation. They tackled Ryan full force, causing him to stumble back in order to catch them.

Damn the man, his smile, and his caring and protective nature. He made her heart do stupid things. Her loins getting twitchy was one thing. Her heart was an altogether different thing.

After garnering his kisses from Alma and Alisa and shaking hands with Khani, Ryan's gaze found hers down the length of the crowded space. He canted his head toward the open front door, and then bound out. Piper stood, skirted the lip-locked couple, and headed for the dirt.

"Take care of him. He'll take care of you," Sloan called after her.

"What if I don't need taking care of?" Piper asked, walking backward and facing the woman and her hunky husband.

"Look," Sloan said, "I don't need it, but I sure as hell like it. You will too, if you give it a chance."

Piper shrugged her answer. Yet, she hurried her footsteps to be nearer to Ryan. To see his All-American face and the graceful authority he possessed over his body. To see his wide smiles and discontent grimaces. To breathe his scent. Feel his touch.

"So, did you enjoy having your ass chewed?" she asked.

They set a steady pace, one behind the other down the narrow dirt path.

"Ah, Khani's just worried I'm thinking with my dick." He shrugged.

"And are you?"

"I'd be in lot better shape, if I were."

"Meaning?"

"Meaning you fuck with my head and the area between my cock and my head that no one has ever messed with before."

Piper swallowed. Her throat was suddenly as dry and scratchy as the ground under her feet. "You're all in on this honesty policy, aren't you?"

"I am."

"Honestly," she countered, "all this talk of dick and head is making me wet."

"Avoiding the topic?"

"Maybe, but I speak the truth."

"I'd oblige you—and me—just about anywhere else in the world, but I'd like to keep our body parts attached for future use."

They ran in silence for a while, their long strides in rhythm, if not sync. The front of the man was a sight, but the back wasn't a presentation to be missed either. His broad shoulders carried their supplies with ease. And that high, tight ass was what her younger sister called an onion booty. Looks so good, makes you want to cry.

"You asked about my family, before. Well, I skimmed at best," Piper stated. "This whole drama started before I was born. While I had no interest in a father, my older sister, Sparrow, lived to know her father. She wanted a man in our lives, in our house. I don't know the details, but my mom was hurt long ago, and refused to entrust herself to a man ever again.

"Sparrow resented my mother and acted out, to put it kindly. The first time she got arrested, I was seven. Blue lights filled our living room. Police banged on our door. I was sure they'd take us all away and shove us into an orphanage. My mom was at work. My grandmother was there, sleeping as usual. She left Sparrow in charge of me and Ivy. We're each five years apart. So, I was seven and Ivy, two."

"It's a wonder they didn't take you," Ryan said.

"Yep. We spent the night in child protective services. To this day I don't think I've ever been that scared. But over the years, I grew to like the cops.

They could at least keep Sparrow in check for a little while."

"What kind of stuff did she get hauled in for?" he asked, and then sputtered and promptly spit to the side of their small path. "Damn bugs!"

They entered the sandy patch of the trail and the stuff suction-cupped her boots with each step. Piper's calves screamed in protest. Her lungs worked overtime. "Petty theft. Drugs. Underage drinking," she panted. "Solicitation. Disorderly conduct. The list could literally go on and on. But it was nothing big enough for them to hold her too long. A minor and all..."

"Sparrow met Matthew Reece senior year in high school and everything changed," she gasped.

"Quit staring at the trail and my ass. You'll get more air in your lungs. Aim here." He tapped the back of his head. "It'll open up your chest."

"In my defense, it is a fine behind and running in place on a smooth concrete floor isn't the same cardio as—"

The unmistakable *whiz* of a bullet whispered in Piper's ear. She tried to scream for Ryan to get down, but her lungs seized. His snarling voice echoed the sentiment first, "Get down." He reached back with his left hand, clamped onto her vest, and went down hard, pulling her along for the ride.

The impact of the fall hardly registered, though it forced what little air she clung to out of her chest. Ryan pulled something from a Velcro pocket on his pack. They were sitting ducks. The realization pounded over and over inside her mind. No cover. No place to hide.

"Cover your ears and close your eyes," Ryan growled.

Instinct ordered she remain alert, but his demand overrode centuries of evolution. Or maybe, it just called to a deeper animal inside. One who recognized the master of its body from the first scent, the first look.

He pitched something into the air. Piper buried her face against the back of his leg, hunkering for what, she didn't know. The *boom* rumbled and rang in her ears, despite her flattened hands. The *whoosh* of the blast warmed her entire body and blew the wisps of baby hairs from her face. Brilliant light made night day behind her lids.

Ryan shifted under her. One. Two. Three. Four. Shots rang out. Piper braced for the rounds of retaliation. But none came. Minus the high-pitched whine in her ear, silence settled around them.

"Are you hurt?"

Piper shifted.

"Stay down," Ryan barked.

She rested her head on the back of his thigh and blinked, trying to regain what little sight she had in the desert darkness.

"The fuckers hid behind the Jeep."

"Oh God. What if Gabrone's gone? What about the laptop?"

"Put the monocular on. Gun up and get ready. There's bound to be more of them and they know we're here. Let's move."

She'd forgone the thermal imagery sight earlier, not caring to see the number of mines and creepy-crawlies they walked among. Now, things had changed. They sprinted the last mile and a half. Adrenaline and dread spurred her. Between the rubble of the jail, garage, and half of a house, a non-bullet-peppered Escalade sat. Its doors hung open like the others, but no bodies littered the ground around it.

Piper tensed, ready to hit the ground at any moment. Other than the curls of smoke reaching the sky, nothing moved. The quiet grew way too loud in her ringing ears.

"Quiet your feet," Ryan whispered back. His fast pace never slowed, yet stirred hardly a trace of sound—that she could hear, anyway.

She tried absorbing the shock in her knees. She succeeded only in looking like the offspring of a strutting chicken and a jackass.

"Strike with the balls of your feet too."

Pride might have won out, had the trick not worked. But with a shift of her weight, she sprang behind him with stealth, if not grace. He motioned her to the side of the house she'd used as cover. They slunk against the frayed brick. The first section only protected their lower halves from an oncoming bullet. Thankfully, the front half of the house remained intact, at least from the outside, and shielded their bodies.

When they reached the front corner of the house Ryan raised his hand. They slowed. H&K close to his face, Ryan leaned the necessary parts around the edge of the house. He waved her on. They stayed against the house, crouching and walking silently. At a window his fist closed. They stopped in unison.

"I can't believe this!" Gabrone's thick Latin accent rattled through the shards of blown-out glass. "There has to be a key somewhere! Look again!"

"Everything is blown to shit, man," another guy said. "I can try and shoot it off."

"And have a ricochet kill me in the process? No fucking way. Go check the bodies. One of them has to have a key."

"Don't look at me," a third deep voice said. "He was talking to you. While you're at it, see what's taking Garcia and the others so long."

How had they missed the explosion? *It was far away, and they were inside half of an extremely large house, and they were screaming like crazy people.*

"What, everyone else is dead and now I'm the bitch?" the errand boy complained.

"No. The Bronce is the bitch and she better keep running and hope I never catch her. If I do, I'll —"

Ryan launched through the low window. Piper reached for empty air, trying to pull him back from danger. Two swift shots split the air. A grunt followed, then metal hit and skidded on tile. Fear strangled her, but rage propelled her through the window.

Her champion? Lover? Whatever he was to her, staggered up from his hands and knees. Blood dripped from his face. Ten feet away, a man the perfect size and shape for sumo wrestling clutched his nuts in one hand. With the other, he reached for Ryan's matte-black H&K, which had apparently skidded a few feet from the guy.

Piper's heart pressed the pause button. She raised her barrel, ready to shoot the big bastard, but Ryan ran at him. Full bore. He jumped, cocked, and then bare-knuckled the man on the bridge of the nose. The crunch echoed in the wrecked formal living area. Sumo dropped like a truckload of salami on a hot summer sidewalk. The man lay as still as the men with blooms of red sprouting from their foreheads.

Was he dead? She didn't know, but she suspected he was. In that moment, Piper realized exactly how lethal Ryan Noble was, and how careful he was with her.

She ignored Gabrone, who lifted from his cringe but remained snug to the side of the hearth.

The rectangle of brick was his only cover from fire. Silver cuffs bound his arm to the metal grate embedded in the fireplace concrete. He'd keep. What wouldn't was her concern for the man who held her heart, for however long or short he wanted it. It beat in her chest, but no longer for her.

Her hands shook nearly as badly as they had after killing the Sinaloa goons earlier. This love stuff was slightly painful and absolutely terrifying business. But she couldn't stop herself from going to him.

Ryan snatched his gun from the floor with his right hand and holstered it. When he turned to meet her his left arm was pinned stiffly to his side. Looking past his bloody lip, Piper saw the rip in his BDU's and the slow ooze of crimson seeping from high on his shoulder. The cradle of his palm warmed her chin and he said something in a language she didn't understand. Then something else in another language.

"I see we'll need to expand your languages," he said in French. Her mouth dropped and he continued in the language. "Listen carefully, my sweet. It's time to put on your game face and make this mother talk. No time for sentiment over silly bullet wounds. Are you up for it? Or do you want me to deal with him?"

"He's mine," she said, not bothering with an alternate language. Let him hear.

Piper crammed her gooey emotions into the recesses and set her fury free. She worked for six months to get to this point. She'd be damned if anyone would take it from her. For two months she'd been close enough to smell it. Today she'd nearly died. Three inches to the left and Gabrone's bodyguard would have ended her life. A few inches more and one would have ended Ryan's.

She turned away from the man she loved. Yep, for better and most likely for worse, she was flipped head over booted-heels for this man. And she turned away from his touch. Away from the draw of him. Skirting another body, Piper crossed to the rather handsome Hispanic. If you took away his career choice, personal disposition, and cocaine habit, his espresso complexion, wide jaw, and even wider shoulders would have been appealing.

He sat on the hearth and puffed his chest, settling her with his eerie black stare. "I saved you from my men. Promised to make you mine. Forever." Gabrone's words ratcheted in pitch.

"That's your mistake. One of many." Piper removed the M4 and ruck, setting them out of her prisoner's reach. "If you'd paid attention at all, you'd have recognized that I am no man's possession. You'd have also seen that I was playing you for information."

"I didn't tell you anything. You're just a cunt. Nothing special." Gabrone thinned his lids to slits as he glared.

"That's not what you said a few days ago," Piper laughed. "But it doesn't matter. What matters is that you're the captive. I have the key. I want something and, as much as it pains me to say this, you're the only man who can give it to me."

"The only thing I'll give you is a bullet." He produced a compact six-round revolver and leveled the silver barrel at her heart. "Neither of you move. You hear me, army boy?" His gaze darted over her shoulder then back again. "Bring me the key, bitch. Slowly, or I'll kill your hero."

Piper schooled her features. "Tell me where Matthew Reece is and I'll bring you the key, without bloodshed. But if you kill him, you'll have to kill me, then you'll never get the key. Dying of thirst ranks right up there as one of the worst ways to go."

"I have back-up. They'll be here soon."

Gabrone scoffed. "However you want to play this."

"Actually, they won't." With his hands raised and palms out, Ryan stepped forward, sidling up to her. "The people I work for coordinated attacks on the Sinaloa's six major facilities tonight. Sure you have men in the area, but they'll be glued to the television, watching footage of El Chapo being paraded in front of the cameras before they take him in to custody."

"You lie," the loyalist screamed. His cheeks flushed as dark as the pools of blood on the floor. His finger wrung the trigger. The impotent *clack* of the hammer hitting an empty chamber resonated. He yanked the trigger again and again with the same result.

One half of the weight of worry lifted from her chest. Like she told Ryan on the HELO, she'd removed the drug lord's holstered pistols, along with the bullets from his back-up piece. She'd stuffed it back in his ankle holster to give him hope, and watched now as it was dashed before his eyes. Yet, knowing all this hadn't made her any more comfortable with having a Saturday night special jammed in Ryan's face or her own.

Gabrone laid the gun on the brick next to him. His nostrils flared with each breath, but his chin jutted in defiance.

"You can't torture anything out of me."

Years of interrogations and never once had the urge to beat information out of a suspect toyed with her resolve. But this guy wasn't *suspected* of a crime. He committed them. With her own two eyes she'd seen him trade people like cattle, send them to their deaths for a profit. Piper drove her foot so hard into his ribs she felt the give of bone beneath her boot. Her fist connected with his cheek in a sweeping left hook. An uppercut followed with her right. Red misted her vision and she didn't know if it was rage or blood. And she didn't much care.

Atop him, she cocked to execute another series of blows, but found her hands pinned behind her back. Piper lifted her foot to strike back and met with a wall of solid muscle. The itch to escape had her bucking.

"Stop, Piper." Ryan's voice was quiet but firm in her ear.

The fight fled her in a second and she sagged against his chest, sucking wind like a wild animal after a death match.

"He didn't have the laptop on him and it's not in the office. It has to be in his Escalade. Go to the car, rip it to shreds, and find the damn thing. If you want anything out of him, you have to let me deal with this bastard." His body pressed her against the wall harder still. "Do you understand?"

"He's mine. This is my job," she growled.

"He's the means to an end. One we won't reach, if you don't start trusting me, Goddammit."

No. She didn't want to let go of Gabrone. He was hers. This was her job. She had sacrificed her career, her cute condo in Playa Vista, and quite possibly her life. Piper turned and stared at the bloody Latino. The man squared his shoulders like she'd given him playful love taps.

"At the rate you're going, you'll kill him before he talks," Ryan reasoned.

"And you won't?"

"For better or worse, this is part of what I do. What I've been trained to do. I'll get you what you need."

Chapter Twenty

Ryan scrubbed his hands. Suds foamed a
thick lather, uprooting the stench of gasoline
embedded in his skin. Through the window
sunlight flirted with the foothills and threatened to
inch the night away. The chase, an endless cycle.
He heaved a sigh. Too bad corruption didn't stop its
endless cycle of amazing him, in the worst possible
ways.

If it weren't for the innocence and promise of
youth...*Alma and Alisa.* For the possibility of good
he gleaned in people and the lives he saved...he'd
have given up hope. Given up this job long ago.

Only psychopaths would get kicks, turning a
starched-backed criminal into a pants-pissing,
blubbering fool, begging for death.

The pilot who'd dropped him into this mess
alluded to the Sinaloa tradition of making soup.
Probably from tales he'd heard hauling military
types in and around Mexico. Cartels made
examples out of those who crossed them.
Decapitation turned heads. No pun intended.
Making soup referred to stuffing a person into a
metal barrel, filling it with gasoline, closing the lid,
and lighting it on fire did too.

As it turned out, a man who oversaw the
process time and again wasn't keen on having the

tables turned. He gave more than Ryan asked for, in return for a swift death.

What Ryan had done should have been the hardest thing he'd have to do all day. But it wasn't.

Not wanting to see the horror he'd created, he left out the front door and walked to the back. Bodies littered the ground and it seemed he couldn't escape himself. He shook his head, careful not to strain his neck too much. After all the activity, the damn graze on his shoulder had finally settled to a dull roar. He didn't want to excite it.

Piper eased the pistol from its bead on his chest, but her gaze followed his advance from where she sat, legs dangling, inside the back of the only unharmed vehicle in sight. A frown and sagging shoulders weighted her appearance.

"I'm sorry," she said. Piper hung her head, but maintained eye contact. "I can see it wasn't easy for you."

"It shouldn't be. The minute it is, I'm done. But it's not the first time."

"Doesn't make it any easier."

"No. It doesn't," he agreed.

Ryan set everything he'd shed to deal with Gabrone in the back of the Cadillac. Gun. Ruck. Vest. A sleek silver briefcase lay behind Piper's fine rump. He sat next to her, biting back a groan as he did.

"Will you let me look at your shoulder now?"

"In a hurry to play doctor, are you?" he teased.

"You're the one who was adamant about staving off infection."

"When we get to Hermosillo you can do anything you want to me."

"That goes against your tendencies, doesn't it?"

"Being shot goes against my tendencies," he countered.

"What's in Hermosillo?"

"Hotels and lots of people."

"Yeah, just what we need, more people shooting at us."

"It's enough people to hide us for a while. Most citizens don't like the cartels in their streets. They've done a good job at cleaning up the place over the last decade. But it's always a possibility," he said with a flick of his wrist. "Are you ready?" If he could, he'd put off the inevitable. He expected her to smother him for answers, but it seemed she wasn't comfortable with the length he had to go to get them. Not that she had any idea. But she'd heard the screams and pleas. No doubt.

"Matthew Reece is my brother-in-law. Sparrow's husband." Piper canted her head toward him, but it hurt too much to reciprocate.

Ryan scooted his left leg into the back and turned his entire body to face her. Damn. So much for a reprieve. Her eyes lightened with hope at the possibility of finding her sister's husband. A sweet half-smile replaced her frown.

"I know," he said.

A little wave formed at the center of her brow. Her smile faltered. "How did you know? Your people, whoever they are?"

"No. Gabrone." A storm gathered on the dim horizon, much like the one brewing in his chest.

Piper's eyes darted this way and that, ciphering facts in her mind.

"Why don't you tell me how you wound up in Mexico in the first place?" Ryan suggested.

"Because the last time I started telling it you got shot."

"You have keys for this ride?"

She dangled them in front of her face.

"Tell me on the road. You drive. I'll shoot, but hopefully, I won't have to."

It took twenty-five teeth-rattling minutes of driving for them to reach the blacktop. Nether spoke during the tense, jostling ride. Ryan cursed the fresh blood trickling from the crescent shaped gash the bullet had carved and every pulse of brain-jarring pain. The torment rippled out through his entire torso. He popped a couple of antibiotic capsules from his first aid kit, pulled one of the packs of iodine solution and a large pad from the bag, and stowed the ruck in the back seat.

"All right, Piper, start talking," he ordered.

"Don't you want me to pull over? To help?"

"You driving and talking will help." He growled the last bit as he yanked the T-shirt over his head. Dried blood adhered the fabric to the edge of the wound. He breathed deeply, braced for the onslaught, and pulled. Braced or not, nausea flipped his gut. "Piper!" he begged.

"Sorry! Sorry! Sparrow met Matthew at some party at the beginning of senior year. He was a good boy from a good family, and my sister set her sights on him. I'd say she was obsessed, but apparently most girls that age spend the majority of their day pining over some guy or another."

"Not you?" Ryan asked before squirting the iodine onto the wound and clamping his jaw shut so tightly it might never open again.

"No." She winced as though it were her he worked on, shook her head, and then continued. "I was too busy with volleyball and making sure Ivy focused on her grades, not boys."

Ryan sagged in the seat, holding the gauze to his shoulder. Visions of Piper in a bathing suit, stretched out and leaping to spike the ball, eased the sting. "Please, tell me you wore a string bikini."

"Perv." She slid him a sideways glance and smiled. "Only when I played on the beach."

"You're doing it on purpose, aren't you?"

"What?"

"Making me tent my pants. I mean, it is an effective form of pain control."

"You're kidding, right?" she scoffed. "How in the hell could you get wood with a bullet in you?"

"It's not in me. It's only a graze. But, Piper, so long as a bullet doesn't kill me, you could get me hard with a smile or a scowl. The memory of your sweet body does things to mine."

"Anyway." Piper cleared her throat. "Sparrow flipped a switch and became little miss prim and proper in hopes of impressing Matthew. It worked, of course. She's curvaceous and fun loving. Easy to love, when she was with Matt. He dulled her jagged edges. Calmed her restless spirit. By freshman year they were official. They married straight off the graduation line. Bought a house just off the beach near my mom's shop in Venice."

"So, when you said from a good family, you meant from a rich family?"

"His parents are some of the best people I know. So, they're good and rich. Not a combo you find every day. They welcomed Sparrow, all of us really, with open arms."

"All right." He eased the gauze from his trap. With only the dashboard dials for light he couldn't see much. The iodine soaked the back of the gauze. Or was that blood? Hard to tell in the low light. But he didn't dare turn on the interior lamps. He recovered the hole, taped it, and set about easing his shirt back on.

"After a year, or at least that's what I gathered after the fact, they started trying to have kids. For whatever reason they weren't successful after another year of trying. According to Matthew, Sparrow went wild, started picking fights, going out until the morning, staying gone for days at a time. Reverted to her old ways. Only this time, she had the means to do it up right."

The steering wheel leather beneath Piper's grip squealed in submission. Ryan reached for her, but the pain bared its teeth, sinking to the marrow. His good hand gripped the edge of the seat. Sheer will to touch her, comfort her, powered his ability to close the distance between them with a hand to her shoulder. But he couldn't hold it there for long. Every muscle in his outstretched arm shook.

Piper loosened her chokehold on the wheel. The white of her fresh bandage showed beneath the sleeve of Khani's spare BDU. She slipped her silky fingers between his and curled them around his hand. With a flash of copper from under her lashes and the softening of her taut mouth, she lowered their intertwined fingers to his thigh.

"I've never held a guy's hand before. Not like this anyway," she whispered after a mile of silence.

That tidbit did devilish things to his pride and cock. Her hand was so close to his crotch. "Keep talking, sweet, before I get any more ideas about what I'd like to do with this pretty hand of yours."

"Nobody has ever pinned *me* with the endearment 'sweet'."

"I like it. Under all those muscles and all that attitude...you're deliciously caring."

Her laugh eased his breathing.

"It would have been easy for Matt to walk away, but he stuck by her. When that alone didn't work he hunkered down, cut off her money supply, and got them into counseling. Even bought her a puppy." She sighed. "Things were better for a while, but Sparrow is Sparrow. All it took was the mention of adoption and she skid, only this time, there was no easing off the brakes. She got hooked on cocaine. He sent her to rehab. When she got out, Matt only allowed her enough money for necessities.

"That's when the Sinaloa came onto the scene. After she sold every valuable not screwed into the foundation, she started trading them information for drugs."

"How'd you know about the cartel?"

"I'm a cop, Ryan. Was a cop," she corrected. "I followed her on occasion. We were working with the local F.B.I. to eliminate the ring. Don't know why I bothered."

"Because you care about her."

Her eyes watered in the muted light and she cleared her throat. "Six months ago, Matthew went missing. We used to talk two or three times a week, and then nothing for several days. I went to the house and neither of them were there. All his clothes were accounted for, car, wallet, and keys."

"Struggle?" Ryan asked.

"At first glance, everything was in its place. But the glass in a frame on an entryway table had been removed. When I opened the back I found two slivers. I finally found Sparrow powdered out of her skull at some hooker's house. She just kept saying, over and over, 'Matt's gone and he's never coming back.' She didn't file a missing person's report. I didn't either because I knew nothing would come of it. So I started my own investigation, used F.B.I. intel and informants. Really screwed myself professionally. But..."

She sniffled and swung her head back and forth. "He wouldn't have left without telling me. Without saying goodbye."

"You have a thing for him?" Ryan asked, keeping his voice quiet.

"No," she snapped. Her fingers unlaced from his and returned to the wheel.

He could have held her there. It'd have hurt like hell, but what was the use. She had to want to be there with him. She wiped her eyes and straightened in the seat. Morning light seeped into the cab through the heavily tinted windows.

"It looks that way. And maybe it is. But not for the reason you think. And not that I would have been willing to admit it, until you went all philosophical on me. 'The absence of something doesn't mean it can't hurt you.' That's what you said. As hard as Sparrow fought for a dad or some male figure in her life, I fought to keep one out. Then Matt came into our lives. For Sparrow he was the anchor she always wanted. For me he was the stability and brace I never knew I needed.

"He took some of the weight off my back. When I needed to vent and didn't know it, he listened. I set out on this misbegotten journey telling myself it was to save my sister's husband. But I need to bring home the brother I miss desperately."

Chapter Twenty-one

Ryan's gaze had been on her for the last ten miles. She'd done a great job of watching the road, the pedestrians, the signs, the neat rows of trees planted in the median. She had a dreaded feeling she knew where their conversation would lead next. The expression on his face when he came out of the half-exploded house said it all. But she wasn't ready to go there. So, she looked at everything except him. That's how she spotted the maroon rectangle and white F for the Fiesta Inn.

Piper parked on the road toward the back of the hotel and turned off the car. With nothing else to occupy her gaze, she relented and turned toward him. His crystal-blue eyes flitted about her face, studying. He met her gaze and, Lord save her soul, he smiled.

"In the back and strip," he ordered.

"Excuse me?"

"Can't have you going into this fine establishment in digital camo and a visible sidearm. Khani packed you some things." He jerked his head toward the back.

"What about you?" she scoffed.

"Bloody camo draws the eye even more, so I'll save my change-o-clothes until I'm done bleeding, thanks. Back you go. Unless you don't mind giving anyone who walks by a show. If you stay, it'll be easier for me to look."

"I'd punch you in the shoulder, but it'd actually hurt." She flashed him the most sarcastic smile she could muster in the face of his masculine beauty. "I think I'm showing great restraint." She maneuvered atop the console.

Ryan's good arm shot out, latching onto the back of her belt. She stilled on hands and knees, ass in the air. Her entire body flushed with heat that enlivened her girly bits.

"I'm showing great restraint." His rough voice filled the confines of the SUV. It slipped into her ears like chocolate-covered strawberry on her tongue, the textured notes a potent aphrodisiac.

His hand slipped over her rump, traveled the ridge of her crack, and set her clitoris on fire without a touch. Thick fingers spread between her legs and pressed into her thigh.

"Careful, my gun is loaded," she said, and giggled.

"So is mine." His hand came down sharp, but not too hard, on her cheek. "Go on, before I change my mind."

She moaned, but continued into the back and changed with his hot gaze searing her skin. Ryan and his team thought of everything. Using Khani's counterfeit credit card and Sonoran-issued driver's license, she had no problem renting a room on the first floor at the back of the hotel. No, she and the scary woman didn't really look alike. Khani wore a face-full of make-up and had the complexion of a porcelain doll. But they were about the same height and build. And in the photo her hair was pulled back and her face tanned. She wondered what kind of photo-shop technology they'd used to make that a reality.

By the time they got the equipment, bags, and Ryan in the room without drawing an army of miscreants down on their heads, Piper could have dropped into the queen-sized bed and slept for two solid days. On top of the sheets. In all her clothes. Even the boots. Instead she turned to Ryan, grabbed his good arm, and pulled him into the narrow bathroom.

He looked at her like he saw the thoughts working their way through her brain as she thought them. A glimmer of amusement twinkled in his eyes, but the signs of fatigue and pain drew deep creases in his lightly bronzed skin. Piper slipped her hands under the hem of his T-shirt. The hard, hot plains of his abdomen and the smooth, snug skin covering his lady-boner-inducing-form played beneath her fingertips. She tried her damnedest not to get sucked into the tidal wave of hormones coursing through her body. *But damn.* When they'd been together she'd been restrained. Sort of. She hadn't been granted the freedom to enjoy touching him, learning the dips and ridges of his torso, the tickle of fine hairs under her palm. She longed to know the taste of him. From the tip of his ear lobe to the tip of his cock.

Ryan stood with his hands by his sides, watching as she eased the shirt up his back. They worked together to extricate his right arm and head, but she guided the fabric over his injured arm with every ounce of grace she possessed. She clutched the shirt and drank him in. The swell of his pecs. The lean cords of his obliques. The bulge of his biceps. The patch on one of his thick shoulders.

Blood tinged the center of the gauze, but didn't soak it. With measured progress, she uncovered a gash nearly two inches long and a half-inch wide. Red and pink marbled the tissue, yet every muscle in her body relaxed a degree. It wasn't as bad as she'd expected. She tossed the bandage in the small garbage can, the shirt onto the floor, and then turned back.

His wide chest, approximate six-foot two-inch height, and those knowing eyes made her feel small. Which at five-foot seven-inches wasn't easy. And somehow, at the very same time, despite everything they'd been through, or maybe because of it, she felt like she could take on the world.

Piper dropped to her knees.

"Fuck. Are you trying to kill me?" Ryan groaned.

While her gaze met his, she wrestled with his laces. "I'm trying to get these big-ass boots off of you. You're covered in mud and blood, and need a shower before your arm rots off." She tugged off each shoe in turn and then peeled off his soggy socks. Feet and sweaty clothes were about as far from sexy as you could get, but something about the act of caring for this virile man, still fully capable in his wounded state, got her hot and mushy inside. She piled his spent garments and stood. Her hand danced over his buckle, but slid around to his gun.

When Piper pulled the H&K from his holster Ryan tugged his bottom lip through his teeth. She swore she'd spontaneously combust on the spot. He was too All-American-hotness and not at all her type. Yet, her body disagreed. She unfastened his belt, eased down his zipper, and pushed his pants to the floor.

"Oh my God." The words whispered across her lips. His erect penis jutted from a neat patch of light hair at the carved V of his obliques. "Commando." Sure she'd seen his package before, but she'd been on her back, restrained, and under attack by his wicked fingers and mouth, and then blindfolded.

She tore her gaze from the biggest, most beautiful dick she'd ever encountered. Her gaze flashed on the shower before being drawn by his clear blue eyes. The whites of his sclera tipped toward pink from a series of burst blood vessels. Hints of wrinkles teased the edge of his eyes and only added to his appeal.

"Can you handle things on your own?" she croaked.

"Nope." He grinned, his dimples pooling deep.

"Wouldn't if you could, huh?"

"Nope."

Piper knelt again, trying her best to ignore his hardening length. She pulled the pants from his legs, added them to the pile, and straightened, confronting his delectable pink head. How in the hell had he fit inside her? Saliva gathered in her mouth and waves of anticipation rolled through her veins. How would he fit in her mouth? Her heart became a jackrabbit, slamming her sternum as though it was already doing what she wanted to do. Pound it out.

"Please," she begged.

The muscles in Ryan's arms flexed. "Let your hair loose. Then suck me off. Nice and easy to start," he warned.

The order made her impossibly wet. She stripped the band from her hair and freed the braid, watching him as she did so. Which revved her engine—and his from the looks of things. His penis flushed red and bobbed in front of her face. When hair fanned over her shoulders she licked her lips and fisted his shaft. Or, at least, she tried. Her fingers couldn't meet around his girth.

She glided her hand over the impossible discordance of satin smoothness and granite solidity. His mouth slackened and a quiet moan bled from his throat. Piper licked her lips. Using both hands, she guided him. His supple tip buffeted her mouth. Relaxing her jaw, she opened wider and popped his crown inside.

Holy shit.

There was no swallowing him back. Hell, not much more than a third of his length would fit. But the exhilaration of the challenge spurred her. As requested, she stroked easily, giving her jaw time to adjust.

Her hair curtained over both sides of her face, creating a tunnel vision of his sex. It worked for her, but apparently not him. Ryan guided his fingers through her tresses and against her scalp. He cradled her head in his big hand. The contact anchored her physically and emotionally. It radiated lust, but attentiveness too.

Together their tempo increased. She sucked and pulled. He pushed and groaned. Moaned. Panted. The noises he produced tweaked her nipples as though his fingers had incited her. Tears gathered in her eyes and breathing was difficult at best. Still she tortured him with her tongue and drove the pace higher.

Piper firmed her grip and worked his shaft. His hair tickled her fingers and she pumped him. The hand in her hair, always so gentle, fisted. Ryan's hips, always still, pistoned, the cords of his abdomen rippling from the effort. When his left hand grabbed her head she knew he was lost to the pleasure.

"Oh. Fucking. Sweet. Mouth." Each word timed with a thrust until he seized.

Hot spurts filled her, nearly choking her with the bulk of his semen, but she swallowed despite his large head stretching her jaw. Salty and a little sweet. Kind of like the man. Again and again she swallowed, relishing in the glory of his pleasure.

After a moment he pulled from her lips. The muscles and tendons in her jaw screamed. The pad of his left thumb scrubbed her swollen lips. He knelt before her, wrapped his right arm around her, and pulled her to stand. His lips kissed a trail from her jaw to her lips and then over to the other side. The gesture, though sweet, did nothing for the orgasm she teetered on just from sucking his cock.

Seeming to read her mind—as always—he stepped back. "Strip."

It took less than a minute to wrestle Khani's clothes from her body. She stood, tiny breasts arched toward his heat, ready for anything.

"Sit on the counter and face the mirror."

Dumbstruck, she stared at him. The sweat of his brow. The mud smudged on his face. The blood on his neck. Those damn full lips. Sit on the counter. Sure. Why in the world would she face the mirror?

"Now, Piper," he snarled.

She turned her stare from him to the waist-high fake marble top. *Smack.* The crack of his hand meeting her bare ass snapped her out of the trance. *Trust him.* Piper faced him and flashed a glare as she levered her cheeks onto the cool surface. She swung her legs onto the counter and turned. Her long limbs made the task difficult. Too much leg to fit in the narrow space, she crossed them out of instinct and sat straight.

Wow. Every bit of her was on display.

Bronze waves cascaded down her back. Tear-puddled eyes peered back. They matched her hair color, but reddened on the whites like Ryan's. Swollen lips, both top and bottom, bloomed like rain-soaked flowers. Her nipples peaked, dissident and flushed.

The heat of Ryan's chest touched her back. Their skin, coated with a sheen of sweat, suctioned together. She found him in the mirror, but he shook his head.

"Look at yourself. How eager you are. How damn sexy. Relax back on me."

Piper let go of everything and trusted him.

"That's it, sweet. Give me all your weight."

She reclined on Ryan's chest. His broad shoulders were visible on either side of her. Her head pillowed on his right pec. Above her, his head canted toward the left, his hot gaze intent on her reflection.

"Play with your nipples," he rasped into her ear. "I'll take care of everything else."

He slipped his right arm under hers and glided across her ribs, down her abs. With his pointer and ring fingers, he spread her labia wide. The chill of the marble wafted onto her little nubbin. Careful not to touch it, *damn it,* Ryan slipped the tip of his middle finger into her channel.

Every nerve in her body knotted, but relaxed too soon since he stopped at the first knuckle. Piper watched in rapt amazement as he pulled cream from her pussy.

"Wouldn't do me any good to tell you how wet you are. You can see it."

Ryan coated her clit with the moisture. It glistened under the intense light. Piper watched her nub swell with his attention and flush dark red.

"Oh God," she breathed.

"Oh *Ryan,*" he growled.

He thrust his first three fingers into her cunt and pumped deep. His width stretched her electrified tissues. Time and again, his knuckles disappeared into her only to reappear slicked with her desire.

"Ryan." She rocked her hips forward on the moan.

"Your nipples, Piper."

She teased her left nipple, flicking it and squeezing the erect tip. His arm did a great job of abrading her right.

His fingers sank deep and stayed. He curled the tips against her vaginal wall. Piper fucked his hand, rubbing her clit on his palm. She pinched her nipple mercilessly. A choked scream filled the bathroom and it took her a minute to realize it was her voice. Hoarse, lusty moans followed. "Ryan. Ryan. Ryan." He worked her orgasm to the end, and then used his wet fingers to cup her sex.

The gesture seemed oddly possessive and, at the same time, protective. And both set one more aftershock quaking through her body. When she went limp he wrapped her in his arms. In the mirror she saw pain draw his features.

"Your ar..."

"Shhh," he quieted.

They stayed locked like that, both bare and spent, until the drum of their hearts settled. Together they showered, her washing them both. She cleaned his wound and reapplied a bandage. Then he took her to bed, curled his warm body around her, and slept.

It took Piper a while longer to settle. The sun streamed in through the edge of the curtains, and she wasn't a napper. Not that they'd gotten much sleep the night before. The containment that relaxed her muscles also troubled her. She was finally free. She had all the means to find Matthew. And, yet, she fucked and snuggled like nothing else mattered. Like tomorrow the world would end.

Chapter Twenty-two

Ryan fell into a contented sleep. Piper snuggled his hand to her chest and nuzzled her bottom against the front of his hips as though she couldn't get close enough. Which was perfectly all right by him. He didn't have much experience actually sleeping with women and he'd found the most peaceful sleep tangling his body with hers. But it wasn't long before the intermittent shuffle of her legs and shifts of her head roused him enough to sense her unease. He allowed himself forty-five minutes. Shit, he could use a lot more, but he needed at least that to be useful.

"What is it, sweet?"

She rolled toward him and smiled. How much she'd changed in the little while he'd known her. Or perhaps, she hadn't changed at all, but let her prickly spines retract, sometimes, and soften for him. Letting him close. Like now.

Heaven knew she'd incited a shift in him. One he'd already set into motion before meeting her, but at his pitiful pace, he may have never realized the change without her. Ryan never imagined sticking up for what he wanted, pushing a women to tears, even for her own good. After his sister's death, he'd lost the ability to speak up, and for good reason to a kid's way of thinking. But he wasn't a kid anymore and it was about damn time he stopped acting like one.

Ryan smoothed her brow and laid a kiss on her lips. Nice and chaste.

"Thank you," she exhaled.

"Thank *you*," he returned.

Her mouth pursed and he kissed her again, longer this time, molding his lips to the curves of hers, tasting her sweetness. He tightened around her, buried his head in her hair, and inhaled her clean scent. Ryan figured he could live to one hundred and never be as content as he was in this moment. Even though he knew this peace wouldn't last, his mind flirted with the word 'love' while his heart stuck a flag in the dirt, claiming the painful and yet overpowering feeling of adoration.

"Why on Earth would you thank me?" she asked, the heat from her breath tickling his neck.

He eased her back, until he could focus on her vibrant eyes. "You first."

"For setting me free. For helping me when I didn't want it. For making me see it's okay to need it, from time to time." Her palm skated over his face, petted the bit of scruff on his chin.

He was about to get mushy and answer her question, but one of his own suddenly took precedence. "Piper, where does your family think you are?"

"I told Ivy and Mom I was going to find Matthew. Sparrow is in rehab, and will be for a long, long time. So, I didn't say a damn thing to her." Her brow lifted, as if daring him to argue with that final point.

He couldn't argue with locking Sparrow behind bars. Hell, after this mess they might just throw the key into the Pacific. But he had cause from a different aspect. "And they let you go?"

"I may be submissive in your bed, but, in case you hadn't noticed, that's the only place. When it comes to my family I'm the dominant."

"Oh, I've noticed. If I notice any more, you'll be flat on your back in seconds."

She shoved at his chest and sat. Her mouth formed an O and she clamped a hand over it. "Your shoulder. I forgot. I'm so sorry."

"It's fine. Feels much better with all the sand out of it." He sat too and leaned against the headboard.

Her hand dropped and she exhaled, filling her cheeks like a chipmunk with the air. She turned to face him, bare from top to bottom and completely unabashed. As she should be. Her fingers coiled a small piece of her long hair before she realized what she was doing and slung the lock over her shoulder. Those bright-penny eyes met his gaze and held.

"Maybe it was the trauma of everything we went through. Believe it or not, I've never killed a man or even been shot at on the job. There was a knife fight once, but nothing like these past few days. Months even. Captivity was something I allowed because it was my only means of getting information."

Though the room bordered on steamy, she chafed her upper arms with her hands. "It took a toll. One I wasn't really prepared for. So, yesterday, when you came out of the house, I knew Gabrone told you something bad. I could see it in your eyes. I wasn't ready to hear it. But now, I need to know."

"Here I thought I was smooth." He shrugged. His shoulder stung, but nothing like a few hours ago.

The click of her tongue said, 'Sorry to disappoint you.' "I'm figuring you out pretty quickly."

He stalled like a mother fucker. His gaze dropped from hers, roving her naked body and finding a birthmark in the shape of Italy on her ribs. The discoloration darkened only a shade more than her light espresso skin. Considering the thing nestled under her right breast, it was a wonder he hadn't noticed it yet. He still had so much of Piper left to discover, if only she'd let him.

Shit he hated when a woman cried. He could let her go on believing the assumptions she'd made, but she was finally beginning to trust him. And then, there was the whole him-becoming-a-better-man thing.

"Damn it, Ryan." Piper shot from the bed. Feet planted on the tan carpet and hands on hips, she hollered. "Just say it. If he's dead, just say it!"

Way to go asshole, now she feared the worst. Not that the truth was much better. He stood and went to her, securing her arms in his grip to keep her from fleeing.

"Matthew is alive."

The tension in her rigid shoulders ebbed. She sagged into his grasp before a thought skewered her hope. Those keen eyes searched his face, her lashes fluttering with her roving gaze. "Is he hurt? What? What is it?"

Ryan turned her butt to the bed and walked her backward until her calves hit the side and she sat. He knelt at the cliff of her knees and released the words.

"On the contrary. He's been well cared for. In six months' time a ransom demand was to be presented to his family with his index finger as proof of life."

Her hand clamped over her mouth, stifling a cry.

"He was given to a farmer under Gabrone's control, told to make him work but not to harm him, that he'd be collected in one year."

"Where?" she mumbled through covered lips.

"Why is the better question," Ryan challenged.

"Why? I don't know why. Why do they do any of the shit they do?"

"You know the answer, Piper. You just don't want to know it. Think. Who was Matthew's only tie to the Sinaloa?"

"Sparrow." As she said the name her head shook in violent opposition. "No, she wouldn't. They took Matthew because of her, but she couldn't..." A sob broke her sentence. Both her hands clamped over her face and she shrugged off his touch. "No. No. No." She screamed into the barrier, but the denial echoed in his skull. The muscles in her arms flexed and she vibrated with anguish and rage.

"She'd amassed half a million dollars of debt with the US faction. Matthew cut her off financially. He was well off, but came from a rich family. They knew it. When they offered the deal it was too good to pass up."

Her stubbornness buckled as well as her middle. Her forehead sank to his chest and he held her tight with one hand at her nape. Tears tickled his chest and broke his heart, while her closeness healed it.

"Sparrow sold him in exchange for her debt and a job, collecting and distributing information for the Sinaloa in the States."

Her wails shook his frame. Left him feeling as helpless as he had the day his sister died. But he wasn't helpless. He scooped her against his chest and took her seat on the bed. Back and forth he rocked her. Comforted her.

"You're going to hate me for saying this," she hiccupped.

"Nah." When he shook his head she burrowed her face under his jaw.

"I wish Sparrow had died. I've thought it before. But now... And I hate myself for wanting my sister dead. You probably hate me too. Your sister is dead and I'm wishing mine away."

"Shhh," he soothed. His guts twisted and nausea threatened to overtake him. Not because of Piper's words, but because he'd thought along that vein for the last several hours. Why had it been his sister to die and not Piper's?

"I just... When we were younger I used to worry so much about getting the call. The call that would tell me Sparrow had been killed in a car accident, raped and murdered, mugged and left for dead. Then I got older. Every time the phone rang, I'd pray it was the call."

She sat and smeared the mixture of tears and snot with a swipe of her hand. Her lower lip quivered. "I just wanted to quit worrying. And that's the only way I knew it would stop. There's a special place in hell for me." Her gaze reached for the heavens.

"Piper, you were responsible for so much more than you should have been at an extremely early age," Ryan growled. "You did the best with what you had. The sister who should have helped you only made things worse. Regardless, you didn't give up on her. You tried and you're still trying for her."

"No, not anymore. I'm trying for Matthew now." She stood and collected the rest of her tears with a swipe of her hand. "Where is he?"

Chapter Twenty-three

"He's being kept two hours away and you're just now mentioning it!" she railed.

"We need sleep, food, and a plan. I'm not risking your life for anyone," he shot back.

"My life? Since when do you think you have authority over my life?" The anger boiled inside her, breaching her high walls, and obliterating sane thought. Ryan wasn't to blame, but he was the only one in easy reach. "You're a fun fuck, but you don't control me. Even the sex has been more trouble than it's worth."

"Stop." Ryan stood, blocking her path to the bathroom or the exit. "You're mad and I can handle it. But you're going to regret this."

"I already do." She planted both hands on his chest and shoved. Nothing happened. "Goddammit!" She sagged to the floor, but his strong arms wrapped around her and lowered them both to the rough carpet. She stared into his tense face, those lighter-than-sky blue eyes. "I'm losing my mind. I want to hate her, but I don't. I don't want to love you, but I think I do." She dragged in a breath. "That's so stupid, isn't it?"

"No, on both accounts." His lips softened, but he didn't smile. He also made no move to kiss her or reciprocate the sentiment.

She groaned into her hands. "Just give me orders to do something, so I don't have to think."

He stood, pulled her off the floor, and kissed her forehead. "Get us some food and lots of it. There's a restaurant attached. See if they do room service. If not, order ahead and go pick it up."

"Wow, I didn't mean playing your handmaid. Unless it's code for something naughty, like my hand on your—"

"If you want to get Matthew tonight, I have to send my people—as you call them—the data from that computer, we need to eat, nap, and then get going. We need time for recon."

He stepped around her and smacked her ass. The playful gesture stung her flesh and rocketed a pulse of awareness to her core.

"Hop to, sweet. If you stand there much longer, I'm going to die of starvation."

She turned and crooked a brow at him.

His large hand snagged the laptop case from beneath the bed and set it on a small desk. He curved a smile for her. "Because I'm going to fuck you until I prove it's worth the effort."

"Sorry," she mouthed.

"It'll take a lot more than that to hurt my feelings or make me leave, Piper."

He opened the case she'd jimmied earlier that morning and slipped the silver laptop from its nook.

"Unless you're some sort of computer genius, you're not getting in." She pulled the pre-shower T-shirt over her head. "I tried for forty minutes while you were busy with Gabrone. It's password protected and then some."

His smile got Steven-Tyler big.

Bullshit. Sure it was stereotypical, but no way could someone look as good as he looked, do the kind of work he did, and be a technological whiz.

* * *

Well, it was a damn good thing she hadn't put money on the bet. Sure as shit, she shoved the door open with her hip, carrying one brimming bag of authentic Mexican take-out and another full of bottled waters, and found Ryan lounging on the bed. Hands behind his head, he watched the upload progress bar stretch across the screen in tiny increments.

"How? How in the hell are you computer savvy too?" She set the bags on the table and threw her hands up.

Ryan angled his head toward her. "I was big into sports, until Rebecca died. Then I was into staying quiet and out of my mom's way. Any time I made a sound she'd hover and smother. Computers were quiet."

"Makes sense." She fought back the guilt of her earlier words. Sorrow also pinched her heart as she imagined Ryan as a young boy, trying to navigate grief and loss when his role models didn't do a very good job of it themselves.

Piper arranged their meal on the table, bowed, and swept her hand through the air. "Dinner is served."

He rolled from the bed and pulled on a pair of boxer shorts from his bag. Like a gentleman, he dragged the chair from the table and offered her the seat before walking the two feet to his side and sitting.

"Enjoy."

"And you," he nodded.

At that point, most anything would have tasted great. But the warm tortilla drizzled with cheese sauce and filled with rice and beans took her breath away. It had been a while since she'd gotten domestic. As far as she was concerned, this was twice she'd fixed Ryan lunch. She hadn't cooked it, but the overwhelming warmth of caring for another human being settled over her skin. It combined with the heavy meal and sleep deprivation to weight her lids.

When Ryan cleared his throat she was well on her way to her fifth heaping bite. Piper smoothed her mouth, afraid he'd found a stray dollop of cheese on her lip. Finding no crumbs, she searched his gaze. That mischievous grin bloomed. One of his soft tacos had vanished along with two-thirds of another.

"You like it?" she asked.

"A lot. Too much, actually."

"Don't know how you can like Mexican food too much."

"I'm not talking about food." His thumb and index finger toyed with his lower lip, drawing her deeper.

"What then?"

"You love me." Statement. Not a question.

That sure as hell roused her. Piper's pulse skyrocketed and her nerves shook like someone set her to vibrate. "That's not what I said," she wheezed on a shard of chip.

That index finger tapped on his pursed lips. "Not in so many words. No. You said, think. You don't want to love me, but you think you do. If there's anything I've learned about you over the past few days, it's that you're a confident woman. Sure in your goals, your body, your mind, your heart. Sometimes your mind just needs a minute to catch up with your body and heart."

She blushed clear to her gooey center. "Eat your food, so we can finish your check-list and go, please."

And go. Those two words hurt just as much as learning of her sister's betrayal. Because after they went, after they completed the goal she'd been desperate to reach for the last six months, she may never see Ryan again.

He shoved the rest of his second taco down the hatch and drank the entire bottle of water in a long gulp. The lean muscles in his neck worked. His Adam's apple bobbed. Soon Piper found herself gulping too and it had little to do with the third of a burrito in front of her.

"If I have to eat, and can't talk—which is one of my favorite things to do, besides you—you have to eat too," he insisted.

After they both finished, Ryan cleared their mess, clicked on the computer awhile longer while she paced, and then set the thing back in the case. "Everything they had is ours. Talk about a bad day to be a part of the SF." He fidgeted with his watch, and then held his hand out toward her. "We have six hours to sleep."

When she reached out he drew her close. His hand locked around her ponytail and he caressed her with a kiss. Hard slabs of muscle met her fanned fingers as she slid them around his torso. The rumble of his chest eased the last of her reserve. He tugged the band from her hair, setting the strands free as he had every other time they'd pleasured one another.

He levered her back and lifted her shirt over her head. "That leaves one for love-making, but I could be convinced to cut our nap back. If the argument was compelling enough."

She reached for his boxers to bid her case, but he pinned her forearms in his hands. "Me first."

Her body coiled at the command. At the authority in his grasp. It injected carnal lust into her blood and hazed her vision. She fluttered her lids in acquiescence and he released her arms at her sides.

"Don't move, unless I say."

"Yes," she moaned.

Like lightning he struck, flicking her clit with his middle finger. "I need a sir to go with that."

The shock slammed into her sensitive flesh, searing the tip for a fraction of a second before the bolt morphed into pure pleasure. It coursed over her nub, bathing it in electricity. "Oh, Ryan," she panted. "Yes, sir."

In tandem her nipples barbed. His mouth sealed over, latching on as though he were thirsty from days spent in the unforgiving desert. After an exquisite minute he released her breast and moved his head to just below her lobe. He sucked hard and her head fell to the side, giving better access. His teeth scraped her skin, then licked and sucked the sting away.

Piper rubbed her breasts against his hairy chest, rocked her hips into the massive bulge behind his shorts. When she found the angle and rhythm that promised her orgasm in seconds he released her neck and stepped away.

"Middle of the bed on your hands and knees. You teased me with that fine ass in the Cadillac. It's mine now."

"Yours as in..." Not wanting to say the words, she let the sentence hang.

"Mine, however I want it. Right?"

She crawled onto the bed, poked her bottom into the air, and looked over her shoulder. "Yes."

The *crack* echoed in the sparsely decorated space and in her head. A sting from his swift hand licked her pussy. She rocked against the sensation, stoking the heat into an all out blaze. Her lids closed and her head craned toward the sky. "Yes. Sir. Yes. Sir."

"It seems you enjoy that a little too much. I may have to change tactics."

"No, sir," she whimpered.

His palms spread over the swell of her cheeks while his fingers hooked in the curve of her hips. The bed sagged under his weight and his thighs met with the backs of hers. His bare cock nestled in the crack of her ass. Awareness prickled her skin, raising the tiny hairs from her nape to her mons. Despite her apprehension, she pushed against him and rocked on his length.

Looking over her shoulder, their gazes melded. What a picture he made looming over her. He stalled her hips and eased her from their contact. She didn't dare complain. Especially when he fisted his dick. He stared at her and pumped the turgid, reddening flesh. Once. Twice. His pace steadied and she lost count. The muscles played along his chest and arms. Crimson tinged the bandage on his shoulder, but he didn't seem to notice.

Pre-cum coated his bulbous head and Piper wanted to scream. She bit her lips between her teeth and enjoyed the show, trusting Ryan to make this worth the effort. Several strokes later, he pointed his cock at her and moved closer. The silky lubrication and pliant head circled around her puckered hole, slipped down between her folds to tease her clit, and then back again.

Her head lolled between her shoulders in desperation, and she found a wholly different view of the entertainment. His now-purple head peeked from between her wet lips before disappearing. "Oh, Ryan. Yes, please. I want to come."

"But you don't need to. You'll be insane with need before I'm done with you."

She snapped her head in his direction. "I need to, now. Oh, please."

He rubbed his index finger over his tip, and then skated it over her pulsing rosette. "Are you sure you need to come?"

Adrenaline rode her heart like a jockey spurring his horse down the final stretch. Sweat slicked her palm and she gripped the bedspread. Her tongue swelled. She couldn't speak.

Ryan wedged the head of his cock into her greedy cunt. She shoved back, trying to take him, but his left hand halted her efforts. He fucked her with his gaze while he rolled his hips in tiny waves, taunting her with a centimeter at a time.

"I need to come. Yes, sir. I need to. I trust you."

His finger steadily massaged the ultra sensitive opening of her ass. "If you're not ready, use your word." With that he breeched her, dick and digit.

The invasion left her panting. Her entire body went oddly numb and acutely attuned to those two areas. His thick penis pumped home at a frantic pace, piercing her womb at an angle. The *smack* of his balls against her clit filled the room. The squeak of the bed joined in the chorus. Piper bowed and gave herself over to the experience. The tightness in her ass eased. He worked his finger in and out with slow, measured strokes.

The contradictory paces clashed into one blinding orgasm. The world around her went white and Ryan disappeared from sight. His touch remained persistent. It increased. Bore deeper. Pumped harder.

"Fuck. Piper. Fuck," he roared as he filled her. Overflowed her. His thrusts slowed, but he didn't withdraw. He collapsed atop her, and then rolled, curling around her as he'd done before. "You know, I find I'm harboring terrifying feelings of affection toward you too."

Chapter Twenty-four

What in the hell did that mean? Seven and a half hours and about eighty-four miles later, Piper still didn't know what to make of Ryan's comment. She knew she'd been pecking at the words for far too long, attacking the same simple sentence from this way and that. Life and death was once again preparing to hang in the balance, flap in the wind, teeter off the cliff, and all the other sayings for being possibly fucked. And not in a satisfying kind of way. Time to focus.

Outside, the last shred of light slipped behind the horizon, plunging the desert into absolute darkness. They left the land of streetlights long ago. The SUV provided the only blip in the night for miles around. Its display screen and lit dials combatted the murk.

Even though they'd had to detangle their limbs when his alarm jarred them both from sleep, Piper had made a valiant effort at ignoring him on the long ride. But once they'd turned onto the narrow highway and left the crowded streets of Hermosillo behind, he demanded her hand. Of course, she'd given it all too willingly.

For the first time since they'd climbed into the Escalade, she turned toward Ryan and found his gaze. He'd been on the phone half the time with his super-secret people, talking about super-secret things, but he didn't' seem to worry she'd blab. His fingers tightened around her hand, released it, and then he straightened in his seat.

"Tucker said the vineyard is seventy acres with three structures. The processing and storage building sits near the road and is the largest of the three. We'll clear it first. The main house is on the top of a small elevation, but we'll reach the worker bunk first. It's only fifty yards to the east from processing. Our objective is Matthew. Find him and get him out as quietly as possible. We have no way of knowing how many men the Sinaloa have guarding it. Could be none to twenty. We'll hope they only grow grapes and not weed or coca. Those crops come with way more guns.

"Farms eat up the land in the area. I have coordinates to keep us straight. We'll turn off of Highway 26 in fifteen miles. Two miles from the turn, the vines brush the dirt road. We'll park behind them and advance on foot, weapons ready. We lay low and watch, until I say go. Do you understand?

"No matter what happens, don't go without my signal. If anything goes wrong, get your ass back to the truck and move. One satellite phone stays with the truck. The other with me. Tucker's number is the last dialed number. Tell the operator your name. He'll accept a call from you."

For the first time, fear wavered Piper's conviction. What was she willing to lose to find Matthew? Before Ryan, she'd been willing to give her life for the cause, and still was, but she couldn't stomach exchanging Matthew's life for Ryan's. She'd just found the person who got her, cared for her, and didn't try to change her. Despite the fact that he had. He showed her love and understanding, which naturally shifted her ideals and perceptions. Whether he was firm in his feelings of affection or not, she planned on keeping him around. One way or another. For a very long time.

"Don't give me that look." His lids thinned to a scolding line. "You're the most bull-headed woman I've ever met, but you can't be about this."

Piper simply held on to her shaking hands and followed the glow of headlights as they revealed their path to redemption or destruction. Nerves twisted her bowels and threatened to rattle her teeth out of her head. Never had she been this scared. Fear wasn't her usual response for intense situations. In neither captivity, the damn shoot out, nor walking through a minefield had she been this on edge. But this was different because now she had something to lose.

"Lock it down, Piper. Or I'll go by myself. You're no help to either of us like this."

"I know," she agreed. "I'm working on it."

Ryan switched off the lights as soon as they made the turn. For a second her freak-out level jet-set as they drove through the thick night.

"Thermal monocular," he soothed.

She released an audible breath and sank against the soft leather.

"You're one hot gray chick. Turn this way, I might be able to see your nipples through your shirt."

Laughter bubbled, and then exploded in a release of anger, confusion, and fear. Her shoulders shook. Her belly rolled. "You're crazy." When he stopped the vehicle and killed the engine, the remnants of her laughter died.

Ryan's scruff tickled her lips a moment before his mouth skimmed over hers. Light as a whisper their skin and breath mingled. His hand cupped her nape, hugging them cheek-to-cheek. "Make it through tonight and I'll tell you exactly what I meant earlier."

"Well," she sighed, "that's incentive enough for me."

A rumble permeated his chest. He released her and retreated to his side of the car. Metal slid across metal. Velcro screamed. Fabric rustled. "Here, eyes on."

Piper accepted a hunk of cool metal she recognized by feel alone as a thermal imagery monocular. She pulled on the contraption and welcomed sight, gray tinted as it was. Two M4's and his trusty blood-spattered ruck piled high on Ryan's lap. He handed her one of the assault riffles to accompany the two pistols and four extra magazines tucked away in the holsters and pockets of her borrowed BDU's, which she buttoned so he couldn't see her nipples and get distracted.

"Keys are in the ignition," Ryan said before slipping out of the vehicle. She joined him at the front of the truck to get their bearings.

Rows of vines shone white in the eyepiece with only a hint of black. The shadows were tinted dark like puddles of swamp water. The succession stretched for a mile to the north and east. At the top of a gradual incline lights burned through conservative windows at the main house while the bunk and process buildings stood like dark boxes.

"What day is it?" Piper whispered.

"Saturday."

"Is it harvest time?"

"By the looks of things, past. I don't see any clusters on these tendrils. That's not to say the other half of the field isn't bursting with them. I don't know when they harvest, if they grow different varieties, if they ripen at different times."

"I've never planted a thing in my life," Piper said. "But it looks so quiet."

"It's possible the workers went home for the weekend," Ryan offered.

"What?"

"Gabrone may have influence over this place, but he doesn't run it or own it. Thermal shows no guards."

"So you're saying they'd let Matthew...what?" she asked, jerking her hands to the sky. "Take a walk? Hitch a ride into town?"

"Small movements, sweet. Just because I can't see any roaming guards, doesn't mean there aren't goons in the house. And I have no idea. So let's go find out."

Best idea she'd heard since the sun went down.

Piper fell in behind Ryan, who stuck close to the foliage. He advanced at an easy pace. Several times he raised his fist just shy of his shoulder before he stopped. Like she wasn't completely in tune with his every micro-gesture, every twitch of his ear, every shift of his spine. She didn't see any movement besides Ryan's and the chilly wind rustling the leaves. And still, she could have played the tightrope to any daring Wallenda.

Six yards away from the network of grapes' end, he pointed to the ground, and then hit the dirt. The gravel and dirt pricked her palms as she followed suit. He crawled on elbows with the riffle lying atop his folded arms. Piper locked her fingers over the barrel and butt to keep hers from slipping. Earthy scents of roots and vegetation huffed through her airway. Only feet away from the open space between the three buildings, Ryan crouched, but gave her the flat of his palm. Then he left her, literally, in the dust.

He banked right toward the bunkhouse. The blood pumping through her heart congealed as she watched him vanish around a corner of black shadows. *Damn.* Piper yanked the useless device from her head and strained for any sound.

Nothing.

Time ticked, collecting in a big pile of worry at her feet. She hugged the M4 to her chest, rested her forehead on the stock, and offered a prayer.

A crash brought her head up fast.

Chapter Twenty-five

Ryan melted into the shadow of the long, narrow building. From his vantage point he could see no windows in the process building. When they'd seen it from the distance he'd expected as much. It likely housed large metal vessels, pipes, and oak barrels filled with fermenting grapes. Shrubs and trees hugged the main house while vines suffocated a pergola that spanned the entire front of the garden house. A row of picture windows looked out onto the vineyard. Luckily, the vegetation helped bank the brilliance pouring through the glass to a dim glow around the immediate grounds.

He'd half guessed the bunkhouse would resemble the prison he'd found Piper chained inside. Windowless. Meager. A bit of hell on earth. As he sidled to the exterior, the richness of the wood caught his attention. It matched the main house. Large panes of glass stretched in five-foot increments across the back. Inch by patient inch, Ryan neared the window made black by the night and a profile that radiated no heat. He switched to night vision, a little trick that came in handy, and moved closer still. On the next inhale, he held his breath, so he wouldn't fog the window, and peeked inside.

What he saw surprised him more than a room full of Sinaloa members with rocket launchers and grenades.

Bunks lined the walls, leaving a slender aisle down the middle. Each bed held a mattress, covers, and a pillow. And they were all empty. All that he could see anyway. Ryan maneuvered to get a better look. No one hid in the corners. He moved to the next window. And the next. Nothing looked out of character for a farm. A wide brimmed hat hung on a high bedpost. Work gloves drooped over the other at the end of another bed. Boots burrowed beneath another.

Ryan continued on to the end of the building. Wood *smacked* into wood in the direction of the main house, shattering the peaceable silence. Riffle up, he moved as fast as his boots would quietly take him to the next corner. He zeroed in on the front of the house, searching for the threat. He found another fucking conundrum.

Matthew Reece stomped from the screen door, or at least, a guy with the same body type. Shoving the monocular from his head, Ryan narrowed his gaze. Then again, maybe not. In the pictures he'd seen of the man they sought, Reece was narrow and pale. This guy mirrored Reece's height, but thick muscles filled out his chambray shirt and the sun tanned his hide a deep brown. Of course, six months of outdoor labor could do that to anyone.

The guy strode, hands on hips and mouth pursed, to the farthest side of the porch. He shook his head several times and seemed to search the heavens for answers. *If you find any, let me know.* Reece planted a sizable forearm on a pergola column, continuing his search.

Dropping his weapon to its strap around his neck, Ryan bolted for Piper. It would take all the discipline she possessed to see Matthew Reece and not sprint for him. He'd told her to stay. And boy, if this wasn't the ultimate test of her trust in him.

At the edge of the bunk house he slowed and could have groaned in sweet relief when he saw her outline, laid as he'd left her, under the vines. She peeked from her cover and met his gaze. Pleading radiated from her features. Her hand gripped the base of a grape plant, as if trying to hold herself in place.

Her expression confirmed it was, indeed, her brother-in-law. Ryan pointed to his gun and motioned it toward his side, showing her his palms. Then he gestured at the house. When she nodded he picked up his riffle and prepared for anything.

Chapter Twenty-six

Thump-thump. Thump-thump. Thump-thump.
Piper's heart pounded in her ear. Matthew was
alive. She swallowed past the desert in her throat,
stood on wobbly legs, and adjusted the riffle by her
side as Ryan had demonstrated. The first step
threatened to topple her, but with each stride her
coordination returned. She chanced one last look at
Ryan. He didn't meet her gaze. His focus and riffle
barrel were honed on the man on the veranda.

Her pace increased until she emerged from
the shadows. Matthew's head snapped in her
direction. His arm fell from the post and he puffed
his chest, the breadth of him nearly doubling. He
balled his fist. His feet spread in a defensive stance,
daring her to come closer.

The man in front of her was Matthew Rcccc,
but not the Matthew she knew. Captivity had
changed him. Roughened his smooth manners.
Doubled his muscles. Etched a menacing scowl on
his face. Gave him a damn fine tan. Now he could
actually pass as her blood kin.

Piper took one more step, bringing her
features into the light. As if she'd beamed him in
the forehead with a billy club, his upper body
jerked backward. Frozen, with her stomach in her
shoes, she waited. Just as quickly as he lurched,

he leaned forward. His hand clamped over his mouth and his head swung in a thin back-and-forth.

She broke in so many ways. The independent girl who didn't need anyone, much less a man, admitted she wanted two men in her life. The need for control, every and all day, fled in the shattering of the person she'd been. She sprinted across the stone path, up the steps, and launched into Matthew's arms.

"Piper?" Emotion choked him.

"It's me, Matt. I can't believe I found you." Tears clogged her voice too. She squeezed so hard her muscles quivered.

"How the hell—"

Without finishing the question he ripped her from his chest and shoved her behind him. Had he been his pre-abduction self, he'd have had a hell of a time accomplishing the task. But now strength radiated through him, just like it did with Ryan.

"Matt?" Piper shoved at his back. She wiggled free only because his attention was riveted in front of him.

"Gun," Matt growled.

Her gaze pivoted to find her lover mid-yard and advancing. She grabbed Matthew's arm. "He's with me. He's the only reason I found you."

"Not true," Ryan chimed, still keeping a lock on the door. "How many in the house?"

"What?" Matt barked. His gaze bounded between them.

"We need to move. Now," Ryan whispered.

"I'm not going anywhere." Matt took a step toward Ryan, blocking his path. "And you're not coming up here until you put that damn thing down."

Piper swore her jaw hit the wooden patio. She'd never seen Matthew get riled about anything. Of course, an assault riffle in your face could give a person cause to rile. But for him to place himself in the path of it baffled her.

"I can't do that until I know it's safe," Ryan said.

"Unless you're scared of an old man, a woman, and her young son, it's safe." Matthew glared.

"What about the Sinaloa's men?" Piper asked.

"They don't come here often, only once since the day they dropped me off." Matthew's tone sharpened.

"Where are the workers?" Ryan pressed.

"Home with their families," he answered.

Ryan eased the M4 to his side, but kept it within easy reach. Piper struggled to control her tongue because that jaw on the floor thing happened again. "There are no guards here. You're not chained to a wall or locked in a cell. And you're still here?" Hysteria bubbled into her mouth and spewed out in her shrill tone.

"It's complicated," Matt explained, without explaining a damn thing.

"Explain it on the way. Let's move. We still have a hell of a journey out of here." Ryan rolled his wrist. "Come on."

Piper grabbed Matt's hand and tugged. He didn't budge. She turned her gaze to his hazel eyes. His stance relaxed and the severity bleed from his face. His mouth curved in a sweet, sad smile. "I'm not leaving, Piper."

Her heart plummeted, meeting up with her stomach in her boots. "Why not?" she croaked.

"It's complicated," he said again.

"Complicated? No shit, it's complicated. You were nabbed by a cartel and I've killed people to find you!" Piper roared.

"Not taken," he hollered. His widened shoulders lurched in her direction and loomed. The pink of fresh sunburn darkened with his anger, going molten red. "Sold by the person I loved most in the world."

Shock made her release him. He knew. She'd worried about how to tell him, but he already knew about the betrayal. Tears streamed in earnest against her cheek and she batted them away only to have them replaced by fresh ones.

"Back away from her, Reece." Ryan's quiet voice whispered across the distance, chilling with its simple menace.

Matt stumbled back. He grabbed his forehead, ruffling the floppy front of his once prim haircut. The brown hair, made lighter by the sun, curtained over his fingers. "You killed people. When? Why?"

As it had when Matthew exited onto the porch, the screen door slammed back against the house. Their heads snapped in its direction. Ryan's gun came up.

A young boy's sweet voice wafted though the air, "Matt, lo siento."

Matthew exploded, "No!" He launched himself between Ryan's aim and a nine or ten year old boy. But her lover had already lowered the sights.

The kid's almond colored eyes went wide. Shock and fear distorted his features. Matt scooped the kid into his arms and gave Ryan his back.

"It's down," Piper reassured. "It was down before he was through the door. Ryan would never hurt a child. Never."

Those small, light-brown eyes swung in her direction. His lips pursed, and then curved. "Are you Piper?"

Matt canted his head at the kid, leveling their gazes. "How do you know that?"

It was her turn to have wide eyes, because that was one of the thousands of questions she wanted answered.

The child's eyes veered back to Ryan and he waved. "When you talk about your family you talk about her. One time you said she had hair the color of the bronze Olympic medal. And she has that color hair. It's been a long time since you've seen your family, so it makes sense she'd come visit. But why do they have guns?" Before anyone could answer, he rushed on. "I'm sorry I made you upset, but I still want you to be my papa. Yeah, you have a family in the United States, but we love you more. Momma takes care of you and the other day I saw her kiss you on the mouth. That means she loves you."

Matthew hugged the kid to his chest. His gaze jumped between her and Ryan. "Complicated doesn't begin to cover all of this. Come inside. We'll have coffee and talk, after I put Manuel to sleep." Matt stepped toward the door. "Where are your momma and grandpa?" he asked the boy.

The boy's head shot up. "Mom's in the back, cleaning the kitchen. I'm not tired."

"Then tomorrow you'll have to work harder." He ruffled Manuel's brunette curls and stepped to the screen.

Ryan hustled up the steps. His hot fingers skimmed her face. The contact broke her dumbfounded trance on her brother-in-law and the boy. She nearly fell into Ryan's embrace, burrowing against his chest. Piper clung to the fabric of his shirt for dear life, absorbing his strength and reassurance.

"More and more complicated," Matt said. He held the door open and wiggled a brow at her.

"You have no idea," Ryan countered.

Chapter Twenty-seven

"Santa María, Madre de Dios." Gabriella marked herself with the sign of the cross. "Such bravery."

"I'm going to vote stupidity." The parenthesis on either side of Matthew's mouth deepened. His jaw sawed and his eyes glistened. "I can't believe you did all that for me." He ran a hand over his face, held his breath for a minute, and then blew it out. "Thank you."

Piper nodded to keep from crying again.

The four of them sat on the veranda in a semi-circle, her and Ryan side-by-side facing the unseen vines. Matt and Gabriella faced each other at opposite ends of a coffee table. Señor Varrera, the old man whose family had owned the farm for five generations, and Manuel had long since gone to bed. On the short table between them stood four fat mugs, and a tray holding a pitcher of water and four glasses.

Matt collected his unshed emotions. Suddenly exhausted, Piper relaxed against the cushy chair back. Collectively they took a break from the heavy stuff, looking out into the night. Stars sparkled. Crickets chirped.

Ryan slipped his fingers beneath her left hand and caressed the top with his thumb. The gesture bulldozed her melancholy. But it also seemed to thicken the tension in the wide-open air. Matt shifted this way and that, then cleared his throat.

Gabriella stood and flattened her hand over her ample bosom that even Piper admired. "You need more than coffee after an experience like that," she said in a slightly breathy voice.

Matt sure didn't miss her chest, his gaze raking her body. He shifted again and flung his scrutiny at the stars. When she turned he relented, allowing his stare to follow her petite frame and curvaceous bottom to the door. The hug of her sundress couldn't have helped the situation one bit. It snugged her small waist and swayed with her hips, just so.

Before speaking, Piper cleared her throat. "So, why stay?"

"At first..." His lips clamped and he picked at a thin spot in his jeans.

"It's okay, Matthew. Sparrow is my blood, but rage wouldn't be a strong enough word for the emotions I feel toward her."

Matt laughed, a short, joyless sound. "That's the thing. When I heard the thugs talking about me being her debt, I didn't believe it. Thought, no. Surely, my wife would never do that to me. But..." He smacked his palm on the wooden armrest. "I was hurt. Enraged with myself mostly. For not fighting harder. For not keeping her in rehab longer.

"I finally realized Sparrow is an adult. Responsible for her own choices. I made a promise, for better or worse, till death do us part. The people who made those promises to each other are dead. I gave her all I had and it wasn't enough. Now, I don't feel anything toward her. She needs help, but not from me."

"You gave her the best years of her life. Really. You pulled her back from the brink and gave me the sister I never knew I had. I felt guilty for a long time too, but we can only do so much. She has to want to change and right now she doesn't. We can't let her destroy our lives too." Piper placed a hand on his forearm, hugging it tight.

"Thanks for not making me feel like a total asshole," he said.

"I don't think you possess the ability." Piper patted his hand before settling back. "So the Sinaloa?"

"They told me and Varrera that if I left, they'd kill Manuel just like they killed his father." His palm turned to a fist. "Six years ago they soaked him with gasoline and burned him alive in front of his entire family because Varrera refused to grow for the Sinaloa Federation."

"Oh my God," Piper whispered.

"For a while I didn't think God visited Mexico. But...the old man treated me like a person, not a piece of equipment. Taught me everything about how to farm."

"Quite a task for a rich city boy," Ryan offered.

"No kidding," Matt agreed. "I'd hardly ever touched anything green. Not even broccoli on my plate. The business end was easy to pick up. I actually helped. Taught him a thing or two about bookkeeping and management."

The screen door creaked and Matt quieted, it seemed, in reverence of Gabriella's appearance. She managed another tray filled with a bottle of wine and four glasses through the door and set them on the table with the other beverages.

"Please, let me." Matthew stood, filled the glasses, and doled them out. When they all relaxed back he continued. "The first month I spent angry, the next two I spent working or sleeping like a dead person. Around that time Manuel took an interest in the process. Señor Varrera gave me my first pupil. The best too. He has instincts about the plants. It's in his blood."

"It is," Gabriella agreed. Her thick lips spread into a prideful smile.

Matthew smiled back and Ryan squeezed her hand. Yep, he felt it too. The awkwardness of being in the room, but completely ignored by the deep connection shared by two people. She glanced at her love and could do the same thing, if she didn't have so many more questions.

"So, you can't leave because of Manuel?"

The chair creaked as Matthew leaned forward. He planted his elbows on his knees and gave her his full attention. "In the beginning, yes. But now there are other reasons." His brown green eyes slid to Gabriella and then back. "I'm happy here. Happier than I've been in many, many years, maybe ever. I love the work. It's backbreaking, long hours, but so satisfying watching the seed you nurtured turn into a bottle of wine that will wow an oenophilist."

"A what?" Ryan asked.

"A wine connoisseur," Gabriella said with a smile.

"Ahh." Ryan ran a hand through his blond locks.

"I love Manuel. He's an amazing kid. And though I've tried my damnedest not to, I'm in love with his mother," Matthew admitted.

Gabriella gasped.

After a weighted minute, Ryan stood and tugged Piper's hand. "We've had a long day. If you don't mind, we'll crash in the bunk house and talk more in the morning."

"That'll be fine," Matt agreed with a definite rasp to his voice.

Piper made a move to set her glass down.

"Bring it," Ryan said. He leaned in, grabbed the bottle, and towed her along behind him.

Chapter Twenty-eight

"Are you okay?" Ryan asked after they'd shed their equipment, weapons, and boots.

"This isn't at all what I expected. But he's alive." Piper unfastened the button at the top of her shirt, and then the next, all the way to the bottom as she talked. "Hell, he's thriving and happy. Maybe I should feel upset. He is still married to my sister, but I don't care."

It was all he could do not to rip the rest of her clothes off, much less concentrate on the words coming out of her mouth. But they were important because she was important. The most precious thing in his life. With the will of a saint he tamped down his burgeoning erection and watched the emotions play across her face. Optimism sparkled in her eyes. Concern crooked her brow. Peace pulled her cheeks. And so much more.

She shrugged and slipped out of the long-sleeve shirt. Next her willowy fingers pulled the band from her hair. Section by twined section, the strands loosened with the help of her deft hands.

So much for not getting hard.

"In every way, Matthew has been more of a sibling to me and Ivy than Sparrow ever was. So, I guess, my loyalties lie with him. More than that, it's like I told him, we—Matt, you, me—can't let other people's decisions rule our lives. For Matt it's

Sparrow. For me it's my mother and her inattentive parenting. If she'd been there for us emotionally, instead of trying to prove to the world a woman could do everything without a man, I think we'd have all been okay. But that's her decision and I won't let it ruin me. Not for the right man."

She had him by the balls already. So, the sucker-punch to the heart nearly knocked him over backward off the tidy bunk. Ryan shoved his feet back in his boots, stood, and holstered his sidearm. He shoved his hands in his pockets to keep from touching her.

"Go have a shower. It's small, but clean. Fresh towels are in the cabinet under the sink. I'll be right back." He stepped around her and dug the satphone from the ruck, and then strode past without a look. One glance would shoot his plans out of the air before they got good and formed.

"Never seen you scared before." A wounded quality hung in her voice.

"Not scared."

"The way you're high tailing it after what I said, I'd have to disagree."

With one hand on the knob he relented. Over his shoulder he raked her with his gaze, hovering at her breasts and tilting his head to get a better view of her backside. "Not scared. Excited, Piper."

"Okay," she dragged the word over several syllables.

"Get your shower. Finish your wine and have another glass. Relax. I know you trust me, but I'm going to push you and your trust to the limits tonight."

Her lips parted, but he turned and left before she could question him further. The exterior lights at the house had been turned off as well as the interior lights along the front. A billion stars glittered in the clearing sky, allowing him to see that the tormented lovebirds had vacated the porch. Ten to one odds said they went to bed together. If he didn't have one more thing to tend to, it's exactly where he'd be with Piper.

Ryan hit redial on the satphone and waited for the first beep. "Sierra. Hotel. Echo. Papa. Hotel. Echo. Romeo. Delta. One. Nine. Nine. Six."

After a series of tones the perma-calm voice of Rhonda Merk answered. "Voice confirmation complete. Agent Noble, how may I direct your call?"

"Commander Tucker, please."

"He's..." she faltered, "away from his desk at the moment. May I take a message?"

Surprise gathered Ryan's brow. In all his years at the Base Branch, these were the most words in succession he'd ever exchanged with the meek woman. In person or on the phone. It was also the first time he'd ever heard her voice waver.

"Is Agent Slaughter back?"

"She's inbound, but still a couple of hours out, sir."

"Where's Tucker? Is he okay?"

"Well," she breathed into the line. Ryan imagined her little mouth pursing as she waffled.

"Just spit it out, Rhonda."

"He's still in interrogation," she whispered.

"Jesus, how long has it been?"

"Too long. For him and Ruez."

"I'd worry more about the snitch," Ryan comforted, though his mind reeled. No one ever lasted that long against the Commander. His cold gaze leveled even the hardest criminals in minutes. And if that didn't work, his practiced hands made them despise their own resolve. Not many people lasted in the business as long as Tucker had. But it seemed time only sharpened his skills to a brutal point.

"You're right. He's fine. Everything's fine."

"Are you okay?"

Though recently engaged, Ryan always suspected the woman had a thing for their commanding officer. He'd been glad when a couple of the female operatives took her out to celebrate her relational milestone. Because no way would anyone's fortitude break through the layers-thick wall of metal Vail Tucker placed between himself and any excuse for a personal life.

"Fine," she squeaked. "It's just, I'm used to the chaos of thirty people running around me, trying to save the world. With everyone on mission at the same time, it's quiet here. Too quiet."

"Sounds to me like you need something to keep you busy and I have just the thing, if you're up for it."

"Me? I don't know if I can help, but I'll try."

"Log into the server and—"

"I don't have access. I just answer the phones and get the Commander's coffee."

"Use mine." He led her into the system and through the maze of files. "You're looking for one of the most recent files. I don't know how he labeled it, or if he even did, but search the key words Sinaloa and Gabrone."

"Okay. How about Sinaloa Hub 187 Gabrone Bookeeping?"

"Sounds promising."

"Now what am I looking for?"

"The name Matthew Reece. I want to know who, besides Gabrone, handled him. I need to know any hub and any person who knows Reece's current location. I also need to know who is in line to gain control of the Hermosillo area for the cartel."

"Give me a minute." Back in her no-nonsense mode, Rhonda didn't make a sound as she searched for the information he'd requested. "Okay, give me ten. There's a sea of names and numbers to go through."

"I'll call back in ten," Ryan agreed.

"Great and thanks. I needed something useful to do."

"Happy to help."

He hung up and headed for the exterior shower attached to the front of the bunkhouse. Ryan opened the cedar door. He'd been prepared for a hose and bar of soap setting in the dirt. The sight of an actual showerhead with smooth stones underneath, a series of narrow shelves, and a stack of terry cloth on the high one nearly had him whooping with joy. He slung one towel over the top, close to the nozzle. Next, he set the phone and his H&K—after checking the safety—on the remaining heap. Then he got to work stripping and getting clean for Piper.

* * *

"Izar Torres!" Rhonda Merk hollered the name as opposed to her usual, "Voice confirmation complete," greeting. "He lives in Santa Ana, just south of Caborca."

"Yeah, we drove through it yesterday."

"We?" Her mousey voice pitched up two decibels.

He ignored the question.

"Oh, sorry. I didn't mean to...anyway, Torres also has a house in Phoenix."

"Arizona?"

"Yeah. That's where he is now."

"How do you know?"

"Phone records."

"Nice work. Tucker needs to put you to better use." Ryan winced at the awkward potential for double meaning, but she didn't seem to notice.

"Thanks. This is fun. Now what?"

"As soon as he gets out of that room, tell the boss to call me."

"Oh." Her disappointment dripped through the phone line. "All right, I will."

"Thanks again, Rhonda."

"Oh, wait. Here he is." All the excitement of a new recruit swirled in her tone. "Commander Tucker!" she yelled. "Sorry to holler in your ear, but he was heading for the lockers." A moment of complete silence passed. Apparently remembering herself in the presence of the commander, Rhonda calmed her tone. "One moment, Agent Noble, and I'll transfer your call."

When she put him on hold he laughed, and then snugged the towel hanging around his waist.

"Tucker," the man answered.

"One hell of an informational," Ryan said.

"He's been trained and he's a stubborn, prideful man."

"Aren't we all."

"I suppose. But he cracked. We wouldn't."

"No, sir."

"Still a ways to go though. What do you need, Noble? Extraction?"

"I need a team on Izar Torres."

"Why?"

"The situation with Reece is unusual. Guzman and Gabrone stashed the guy with a family they terrorized for loyalty. They were to retrieve him after a year to make ransom demands on Reece's family. If he leaves, they'll burn a young boy to death for the offense." Ryan scrubbed a hand through his damp hair. "I need all the records of Matthew Reece as a cartel asset erased. Torres is the last with any link to him. I'd do it. Hell, I'd love to do it. But I can't risk leaving them open to attack."

"When do you need it?"

"Yesterday, but as soon as possible will do."

"We're thin at home base, but I can reroute an incoming team. Consider it done in twenty-four hours. Then wrap it up and get back here. I have a mountain of paperwork for you to complete on this joyride of yours."

"Yes, sir. I earned it."

"And then some."

"You heading back into the room?"

"Seems I'll be in there for the rest of my life. He's let off a lot. Copped to knowing about the cargo load you intercepted and two others at a northern site. I had to send teams there too. But he's holding back on something."

"If anyone can get it out of him, you can."

"Quit kissing my ass, Noble."

"Yes, sir." He had a much finer one in mind for that.

Chapter Twenty-nine

Piper licked wine from her lower lip and considered the gulp of burgundy liquid swirling inside the crystal goblet. The oak, pepper, and berry of the full-bodied fiesta settled on her tongue before she swallowed. Her finger rubbed the glass rim. A whine resonated deep in the cubby of the bottom bunk. She relaxed back, part on the pillow and part on the wall. Her feet tapped together in reined anticipation. Glancing across the room at Ryan's glass, she moaned. If he didn't hurry, she'd have an entire crystalline melody prepared. She'd already towel-dried her hair, combed the tangled mass, and even done a few yoga poses to loosen her tight muscles.

Chained to the wall, she'd learned the value of patience. Yet, where Ryan was concerned the skill fled her altogether. She eyed the red ring around her wrist. The cool room soothed the wound. The freedom from the bandage alleviated some of the insane itch the healing process incited.

Done waiting, Piper gulped the last of her wine, set the glass by the wall, and stood to find Ryan. Perhaps her state of undress could persuade him from whatever task he'd set upon. As she reached for the door handle, it swung wide, away from her grasp. The open door displayed a mental feast of orgasm-inducing man. White terry cloth hung low on Ryan's lean hips, accentuating the rigid V of his abs.

The fuzzy warmth of a quarter bottle of wine morphed into fireside heat as he groaned. Anticipation obliterated her breezy calm, riding her neurons like leather-wearing bikers. Her nipples beaded. Piper wanted to beg him to order her around. To tell her exactly what he wanted and how he wanted it. Thanks to him, she knew how to do it without a word.

She walked to the foot of the first bed, opposite the door, turned toward Ryan, and surrendered herself. Mind. Body. Soul. Back straight, shoulders relaxed, Piper knelt and rested her hands on her thighs. Dropping her gaze from his body stung. She longed to watch his diamond-blue gaze rove her body. To watch his muscles tighten in response. Just as her body coiled for his. But the reward far outweighed the temporary gratification.

Out of her periphery she saw Ryan step inside and drop his clothes into a heap. The door *thunked* closed. Step by slow step he walked past her. Higher and higher thrill whirled inside. The gallop of her heart challenged that of a wild stallion. He moved behind her and placed two things on the floor beside the bed. Then the vibration of his breath tickled her ear.

"Like a unicorn or a repeat triple crown, I didn't think you existed. And here you are. So powerful and strong-willed. So beautifully submissive." His big, bare feet stopped in front of her. "Look at me, Piper."

The sparse hair thickened on his corded calves. His thighs bulged with knitted sinew. Veins swelled beneath the velvety skin of the full erection that jutted from his hips. Up his abdomen, torso,

and arms, her gaze roamed. Then over his
shoulders, the scabbing gouge, strong jaw, and
luscious lips. After the visual tour, she landed on
maybe the most precious thing of all. His eyes.
Ryan Noble's honesty and care flowed through
those blues. His mischief and endearing humor,
even lust and sometimes anger, sparked there too.

"I see all of you, sir."

His dimples flashed, and then fell away. "I
don't know if I can ever thank you for sharing
yourself with me. For letting me inside, not just
your decadent body..." He offered his hand, helped
her off the floor, and then continued. "But here."
His lips swept her forehead. "And here." He dropped
to his knees and his mouth pressed a kiss over her
heart.

Piper swore the damn thing leaped out of her
chest. She swallowed past a ball of emotion and
grabbed his face. His heat radiated into her palms.
When he smiled she held the best part of the world
in her hands. Yes, he was a man, the gender she'd
been warned against since birth. Yes, he was a
killer. Yes, he was her hero. He was her heart,
beating outside of her body.

The words played on her lips. Ticked and
tormented them.

"Piper, it's time to put that trust to the test.
Do you remember your safe word?"

I love you.

"Bronce," she said instead.

"Good. Now, go grab the top rail at the foot of
the bed and face me."

"Yes, sir." She gulped in excitement and
trepidation, turned, and walked toward the bed.

"Damn, I actually looked forward to your
insubordination. I rather enjoy swatting your sweet

bottom. But your compliance gets me hard too," he growled.

"You were already hard, sir," she teased. The *smack* sounded a split-second before the sting licked her right butt cheek. Piper gripped the highest metal rail and arched her back, presenting her ass to him. The bold move shocked them both.

"My stubborn woman." Grabbing the metal just outside her fists, he crowded her from head to toe. Yet, only the heat and power of his body touched her. "I know I told you to face me. I should wear your bottom out, but I think you'd enjoy it too much."

She would. Her clit ached and she longed for the bite of his hand on her backside. Summoning all the self-discipline she possessed, Piper straightened and did as he'd asked. When she turned, his face hovered only inches from hers. The muscles in his jaw flexed and his lips pressed into a hard line.

"Is your grip firm?" he asked.

"Yes, sir."

"Whatever you do, don't let go."

She could only nod at the intensity of his stare and harshness of his tone. He reminded her of a lion, circling its prey, sizing it up before the attack. And attack he did. With the velocity of a bullet, Ryan's hand snagged a handful of hair at the base of her neck. The force pricked her scalp. His mouth descended like the second shot from a gun, impacting her mouth with the full weight of his appetite.

Their lips crashed together. Piper firmed her grip to keep from being enmeshed in the metal slats. The loose metal clinked and whined in the upheaval. His lips dominated her own. He pressed her mouth. Plumped it. Scraped his mouth against hers, bumping her nose with his own. He moaned a sweet song of agony. At last his mouth hung over her lips. He breathed in her scent, an expression near pain etching his features and punctuating his gasps.

"Whatever you do, don't let go...of me."

Piper pressed her forehead against Ryan's. "I'm not holding you, but I could."

"You're holding me in every way, sweet. In every way."

"I won't let go. Not even if you order me to."

Ryan devoured her with his kiss. Harsh and infinitely tender at the same time. His mouth roved her neck, slipped between the shallow valley of her breasts, skimmed over her belly. His hot fingers caressed the acreage of her skin. He circled her most intimate parts, but didn't enlist them in the incursion of her senses.

Her fingers itched to plunder the locks of his floppy blond hair and guide his mouth where she wanted it most. But she refused. Instead she focused on his touch. Not what she wanted it to be or what she expected next. She focused on what it was in that moment. In each smoldering moment.

Long strokes of her thighs. Warm suction on her hips. A graze of nails over her ass cheeks. The nip at the inside of her calf. A hand spread wide over her waist. Small kisses skipping each rib.

When he paused, Piper opened lust-heavy lids. Ryan stared at her from where he knelt. He should have appeared vulnerable. Yet, he'd never been more in command of himself, or her. "Turn around, face the wall, resume your grip, and don't let go."

"Never," she agreed.

"Remember you said that."

The tiniest bit of apprehension mixed with excitement, zinging awareness across her flesh. Piper turned. Her fingers glided over the slats. The metal where she'd held fast only moments ago slid beneath, hot to the touch. She widened her arms and the chilly railing greeted her embrace. One-hundred-eighty degrees should make a big difference, lose a bit of the connection. But...

Ryan brushed her long hair to the side and every sense screamed to life. Much like it had when he'd blindfolded her, the denial of one sense enhanced the others. His scent drugged. His simple touches provoked. And those grunts that rumbled his chest and swept his sultry breath across her skin, ramped her need.

"Spread your legs."

She did as he asked.

"As wide as the bedposts, Piper. I want to see every slick fold and greedy entrance."

Despite the niggling fear that she knew exactly where he planned to go tonight and how he planned to push her limits, she spread for him. Immediately, his hand rose between her legs. His steady palm splayed and cupped her mons. She arched against his fingers and cried at the bliss of first contact. Hell, he'd been toying with her for damn near twenty minutes and hadn't even accidentally grazed her goods.

"Do you want to come, sweet?"

"Yes," she begged.

"Then relax your shoulders and arch your tight ass my way." His other hand pressed at the small of her back while the other pulled. "That's it. Relax your tummy and curve your back." He positioned her just as he wanted, and then dropped his hands.

"No, please. I need to come, Ryan. Please, sir."

He clasped the tops of her wide thighs and sealed his scorching mouth over her clitoris. Devilish suction tugged on the bundle of nerves. Piper's palms slicked with sweat. She fought the urge to buck against the strength of his ravenous pulls. Her head sagged between her shoulders and she panted, battling back the orgasm she just requested. It was too much too fast.

Her nipples flushed ruby red on her chest and beaded to the point of irritation. On her thighs, Ryan's fingers indented her flesh. Between her legs, the point of his chin bobbed as he worked. He sat on his heels in the spread of her legs. His chest and abdomen sat on display. In the part of his wide legs, his flushed sex undulated with the easy rock of his hips. The drip of precum leaking from his thick tip and the impeccable timing of his flicking tongue pitched her over the edge without mercy.

"Oh...Ryan. Oh...aahh...aahh." Piper hollered until the breath ceased in her lungs. She was suspended in the white world of ecstasy. Lost to her own body. Lost to the world.

Her grip slipped on the rail, jarring her to the reality of gravity. But Ryan's arms wrapped around her middle. "I have you and I'm never letting go." He secured her to his chest, allowing her to enjoy the gentle fall from post orgasmic oblivion into mad love. When her breathing steadied he placed her hands back on the rail. "Give me another, sweet Piper."

"Yes, sir," she panted.

His fingers tweaked her nipples and already her body started the build. She stretched a little less severely than before, pressing her small, yet amazingly swollen, breasts into his hands. As she settled back, his rigid cock nestled in the crack of her ass. Her hips rocked, milking him with her crevasse, rubbing him against her pulsating rosette.

Ryan dropped a hand to the underside of her thigh and lifted it off the ground. He settled her foot onto the bottom mattress between the wide slats. *Holy Mary!* His hand skimmed higher, and then slid into her wet heat. Piper adjusted her grip and sank back onto his finger.

"God, Piper. You're so responsive. Wet and ready."

"For anything," she goaded, and hoped it was true.

He swept her hair to her right shoulder and nipped her trap. "I think you are." He added another finger, working her pussy in long, swirling strokes. When he pulled out, those magical digits drew a figure-eight, circling her clit and ass entrance in turn, getting closer with each pass. With a generous swipe of her liquid desire, he flicked her nipple and slid two fingers into her compact opening.

A wave of heat swept her from head to toe. Her pulse jumped several notches and her hands quivered.

"Relax, sweet." He stilled his left hand while guiding his right hand through her damp lips. A shock of rapture rippled through her as he flicked her clit, and then massaged the sting away.

Maintaining her grip, Piper loosened her muscles and sank against his chest. When he wiggled his fingers a little deeper, the sensation changed from edgy pain to incomprehensible pleasure.

"Ryan," she moaned, "I can't…understand. It feels so fucking good."

"I have you, Piper. I'll make you feel even better. Just feel."

Her hips rolled of their own instinctual will, while Ryan finger-fucked her ass and tormented her sensitive nubbin. A sheen of sweat slicked their bodies, but neither stopped the rising tempo.

Orgasm sucked her under the surface as surely and suddenly as a rip tide. It tumbled and whirled her until she couldn't discern up from down. Left from right. Him from her.

Somehow she clung to Ryan's neck and burrowed in the security of his arms. Minutes later soft sheets cooled her back. She opened her eyes to find him looming over her. A look of barely contained, lust-filled savagery drew his features, tensed every muscle in his beautiful body.

"Turn over," he ordered.

With excitement akin to an all-expenses-paid shopping spree at IKIA, she flipped onto her belly on the twin bed and raised her throbbing bottom. Over her shoulder she watched Ryan's gaze darken as it strayed across her body. Then he was atop her, only his knees and wrists brushing the skin at her thighs and the sides of her breasts. With his right hand, he pulled her chin farther back and fused their mouths. He tempted her tongue from her lips and sucked it into his mouth. After several pulls he released her, and then returned for more. Their tongues quarreled longer still.

"Before I met you, I was content with my life. Happy in most things, but now I know I had no idea what happy was. It's not smiles and jokes. It's pleasure and pain. Unimaginable joy and impossible fear. It's giving yourself to another and having them give themselves in return." He kissed her lips. "You've given me everything, Piper, and everything I am, I give to you."

She used a hank of his hair and pulled his lips to hers. Stupid tears blurred her vision. She loved his mouth for a long minute, and then levered back to breathe. "I love you, Ryan."

His jaw flexed and something flashed over his face. He placed two fingers over her lips. "We'll see if you love me tomorrow."

"Whether this lasts another minute, day, or decades, I'll love you forever."

The weight of his chest pushed her into the mattress. His palms caressed a path to her hands. He wound his fingers with hers and squeezed, cuddling her with his entire torso. The security blanketing her in that moment topped it all.

When he released her he straightened as much as the bunk would allow and gripped her hips. With his effort they lifted off the bed, plumping her ass in the air and setting her onto her knees. She rose to elbows and braced her quaking body with two fists full of sheet.

The broad head of his cock grazed her supple rose, coating it with the evidence of his raging need. Without another word or further play, Ryan pressed inside the barest of an inch. Piper's body screamed in rejection. The sting and strain bore down even as his hips stilled.

"Relax, sweet, and when you're ready push against me." He soothed her thighs and cheeks with whisper light strokes of his hands. "If you need it, use your word."

It wasn't pride that stopped her from hollering, but a soul-deep need to possess him as he possessed her. To feel the strange and mind shattering release his fingers wrought. Piper let go of her fear, loosened her muscles, and put her trust in Ryan's decisive hands. The pain faded and in its place a bone deep tingle spread.

He gathered her hair from her back, swirled it into a ponytail, and tugged. Her neck arched with the haul. The whole of her scalp became an erogenous zone, coursing a wave of hunger all the way to her toes. "Yes." She pushed against his head and accepted another inch. "Oh God."

Ryan's hands continued to alternate toying with her nipple and drawing on her hair. Sensations stacked one atop the other. Palms now spread wide on the white sheet, she pressed back again.

This time he groaned. "Oh. Piper. Fucking sweet, Piper."

His words whipped her into a frenzy. She bowed deeper, taking him to the base. Sensations reeled and her insides melted into a puddle of want. Ryan moaned as he pulled out the tip and slipped more easily home. Her clit thrummed with excitement.

"Piper, I'm not going to last very long. You're killing me. God. The curve of your hips. The sway of your back. Fuck." His hips rocked.

The brunt of his power and wide head rammed into her with each thrust. Ryan abandoned her hair. One hand clamped onto her hip while the other slid around front. He gathered her desire and slicked her aching bud, circling it like a man possessed. The rhythm rose higher and higher. One more battering stroke and she exploded like the detonations at the compound. Her eyes clamped against the brilliant light. She flew through the air, screaming her release to all of Mexico.

"Fuck. Piper. Oh." Ryan rode out the rest of his orgasm in silence, but his muscles yelled for him, contracting in tight bands all around her and pulsing inside.

Breath by ragged breath they returned from the insane high together. He pulled from her and it was as if he'd given her legs permission to give out. They quivered as though she'd done PT for two solid days. And, in a way, she had. Ryan eased her down and flipped her to face him.

There were no words. He simply kissed her lips, and then lay next to her. With a flick of his wrist he rolled her on top of him, pillowed her head against his chest, entwined their legs, wrapped his arms around her, and sighed. And she felt the same way. Piper hugged the breadth of the man beneath her and passed out.

Chapter Thirty

A noise barged in on Piper's slumber. She snuggled her face into the warmth and tickle-soft hair of Ryan's chest only to have her world tilted on its axis. Her lids flew wide and she bolted upright. Ryan knelt proposal style on the floor and leveled the gun at the bunkhouse door. Her heart shot off like a rocket as she struggled to orient to the unusual surroundings and even crazier situation.

How could she help? Were Matthew or the Varrera family hurt? How many were there?

Before a single question was answered the door swung wide. Manuel and Matthew stepped into the threshold. "Let's go, lazy…" Matthew's gazed jumped between her, Ryan, and the gun. His hand clamped over the young boy's eyes as Manuel announced, "Lunch is ready and Momma won't let me eat without our guests."

Ryan set the gun down while Piper searched for the damn sheet. The freaking thing hung off the end of the tiny bed. She lunged for the pillow instead.

"You can cover your own eyes too, Reece," Ryan growled.

"Oh, sorry." By the time she covered all the important parts, her brother-in-law had averted his gaze. "Hey, we're not blood and I'm a guy. She's… never mind. Sorry." He walked them backward out of the door and fumbled for the handle. "Lunch is ready, whenever you guys are."

"Thanks," Piper squeaked.

"We'll be there in ten," Ryan said, more confidence in his voice. When the door closed he fell onto the bed. A deep rumble of laughter vibrated the mattress. Those teeth gleamed as bright white as the sheet and his dimples hollowed.

Piper reared back and smacked him in the belly with the fluffy pillow. Damn the man, but he only laughed harder.

"Okay, could it have gotten any more awkward. I mean, Manuel is what? Ten years old? And my brother-in-law. Ugh!"

"Hey," he said, struggling for a straight face. "At least I wasn't balls deep."

That was it. She buried her face in her hands and shrieked with amusement. Her shoulders shook. Her stomach cramped. Ryan joined her and before long both their faces streaked with tears.

Maybe it was the break in life-and-death tension and emotional Russian-roulette they needed. They each lay naked in the fetal position on the teensy bed, fighting giggle induced stomach cramps. When at last they subsided he pulled her face to his and laid one on her.

"Good morning," he winked.

"Good afternoon," she countered.

He stood and scooped her into his arms. "By my estimate, we have nine more minutes before we get another rescue party. Shower with me. I promise not to be naughty."

"But I don't." She smiled.

* * *

Fifteen minutes and two orgasms later they raced to the house in the only clean pairs of civilian clothes they had left. Piper's face heated the closer to the house they came.

"Don't sweat it, sweet. You gave a young boy something to dream about for the next ten years." Ryan's grin spread damn near ear to ear.

"Disgusting," she whispered, slipping through the door he held open.

"Sorry, we probably should have knocked first," Ryan said by way of greeting to the four people gathered around the dining table.

Gabriella and Matthew blushed. Manuel found an interesting spot on the ceiling. Old man Varrera slapped the table with his leathery hand and giggled. In Spanish he said, "It's about time these old beds got put to good use."

The couple at the table blanched. Gabriella hid her face in her napkin, which only made Matthew pale all the more.

"Listen, chica." At his place at the head of the table, Varrera stood. He used the table as leverage and leaned to his left, grabbing Gabriella's hand. He removed the thatched hat from his head. When he placed it over his heart the thing crackled like his joints did when he moved. "You love my son. I love my son. But he's gone and it is a beautiful gift to be able to love another. Don't squander it on my account or anyone else's."

He set the hat over his halo of white hair and shuffled right. "Son, stand and give me your hand." Matthew stood and placed his big, strong hand in the old man's well-used one. "If you love her, tell her so, and prove it every day. If you don't, tell her so as to keep from breaking her heart again. Know that if you hurt her, you won't have to worry about Guzman, Gabrone, or Izar. I'll handle you myself. I may be old, but I'm a decent shot."

Matthew glanced at Piper. She blinked the tears from her eyes and offered him a smile. His gaze hopped to Ryan, and then made the rounds to Manuel and Gabriella for a moment longer than the rest. He smiled at Señor Varrera. He surprised her by speaking Spanish. "I love her, Señor. I've told her and I plan to prove it every day. I love Manuel too. And I'm fond of you as well."

"You love me?" the little boy screeched and jumped from the table. His small feet thundered across the wooden floor. Five feet away he leaped toward Matthew. Her brother-in-law lurched forward, catching the trusting boy in mid-air and pulling him to his chest.

"Of course I love you," Matthew whispered.

With all the commotion Piper didn't have time to feel awkward. Now that things wound down her wheels began to creak and squeak. She'd told Ryan she loved him, and she did with everything she had. She didn't say it to get him to respond in kind. Heck, she hadn't even thought about it until the wise man's speech. Life was too short to horde your feelings, or worse, not allow the possibility for them to develop in the first place. Well, she'd come a hell of a long way in a short time. She'd allowed Ryan into her heart. She'd said her piece, and she'd be at peace with it. No matter the outcome.

Varrera eyed her and Ryan. "Same advice goes for you two."

"Sí, Señor." Ryan looped his index finger around her pinky and lifted it to his mouth.

The old man patted his belly. "Now that the kissy stuff is out of the way, come sit, and we'll eat."

Gabriella wiped her eyes and stood. She kissed her father-in-law on the cheek, smiling at

Matthew and her son. "One moment and I'll be back with the food."

"Please, let me help," Piper offered.

Her pretty brown gaze widened on Piper and her smile fell. Still, she nodded. "Certainly."

Ryan released her hand and headed for the table.

As she and Gabriella walked toward the kitchen she heard Matthew. "Red or white?"

Off the dining room stood a gorgeous garden kitchen. Herbs sat in boxes on each of the four windows and houseplants' vines snaked across the cabinet tops. The bowl at the center of the wood-slab island overflowed with fresh fruits and vegetables. Gee, all Piper had were two dead ferns on her back patio and frozen dinners in the freezer. She hadn't had anyone to entertain or cook for in a long time. Still didn't. Not really.

But she'd like to.

Gabriella's brown waves swished about her shoulders as she hurried around the kitchen, stirring pots and arranging food.

"How can I help?" Piper asked.

The woman set the lid back on the pot and turned to her. She opened her mouth. Closed it. Then covered it with her hand.

"It's okay, Gabriella. Just say what you're thinking."

She batted at more tears. "I'm sorry." Her palms smoothed over her teal-blue sundress. "I mean, you must hate me. And—"

Piper raised her hand and shook her head. "Quite the opposite actually. You and your family are perfect for Matthew."

"But he's still married to your sister." Gabriella's hand settled over her bosom. "I'm not okay with that. I don't see how you would be. But I do love him," she rushed to add.

A smile etched Piper's face. "My sister made Matthew suffer miserably for her selfishness. When you betray someone so deeply as to sell the one you supposedly love it makes a marriage no more than a technicality. A piece of paper." She walked around the island, stopping a few feet away from Gabriella. "I know you love him. And he loves you. I saw it before you were willing to admit it. That's why it's okay."

Gabriella lunged forward and wrapped her arms around Piper's neck. No question where Manuel learned the art of physical displays of affection. She smelled of dirt and flowers, was as petite as a miniature horse, and hugged like a bear.

"It's a piece of paper I'd like you to sever for me," Matthew said from the doorway. He stepped into the room and slid an envelope across the table. His fingers pinched his lips, and then he sighed. "You know you're always my sister, right?"

"And you're always my brother."

Gabriella flagged him over with a hand and shoved Piper at him. "Hug. You two are making me a mess." The hand that flagged now fanned another gush of tears.

Ryan strode into the kitchen. "All right, enough mushy stuff." He smiled. "The men are hungry."

"Yeah, they are," Matthew agreed. He kissed her hair, and then set her back next to Gabriella. "How can we help?"

His new love's weep grew to a wail. She covered her mouth with her hand to stem the noise. With her other hand she hugged her arm, until Matthew pulled her into his. Ryan's brow furrowed. Instead of high-tailing it into the dining room, he advanced around the island, stopping only a few feet away.

"You know Piper is happy for us. So, what is the matter, Gabriella?" Matt smoothed a hand over her hair and held her close.

"She is, but the Sinaloa won't be. Guzman and Gabrone are dead, but the Federation still lives. If anything happened to you..." Her head shook. "Izar knows you're here." She wept onto his shirt.

At once the men both spoke. "My aim has improved. I can shatter a bottle at a thousand yards. Now—" Matt offered. "They won't be a problem for you anymore," Ryan said.

Piper and Gabriella returned the favor by gasping, "What?" at the same time.

Matthew turned to Ryan. "What did you say?"

"By nightfall your records with the Sinaloa Federation will be erased," he answered her brother. "As will your family's, Gabriella."

Joy swirled in the room. The lovers said and showed their appreciation in big hugs. But dread sucked Piper into a vortex with no air. This was it. Why he'd told her to wait until tomorrow. He would leave to handle the cartel and she'd never see him again. It made sense, really. She was safe. He'd made her brother and his new family safe. Now he'd crush her heart. Piper hadn't lied. She'd love Ryan forever, but damn, she wanted to like him too.

His warm, wet mouth glided over hers. "It's not my mission, Piper. When it's time, you and I will leave here together."

And then what?

She didn't know, but she wouldn't waste good time borrowing trouble. It would find her soon enough. It always did.

"Ewww. Disgusting." Manual teetered into the kitchen, carrying three wine glasses.

The old man shuffled behind him, hauling three more and a tall glass of water. "I thought we were done with all this mushy stuff."

"I'm sorry," Gabriella offered. She rushed forward to help the men. "What are you doing?"

"Figured since the majority of us were in the kitchen with the food, we'd eat in here," Varrera answered.

When all the bustle was said and done, the old man and women sat on stools around the island while the younger men stood. Manual's head scarcely cleared the wooden top, but he managed to eat and not ogle her covered breasts too many times. His head was at an inconvenient height, though.

Near the end of the meal, Ryan filled everyone's glasses and raised his. "To family and future."

"And the present too," Matthew added.

Chapter Thirty-one

The Varrera's plied them with food, drink, and stories until he was beyond the definite line of gluttony. His face and stomach ached from laughter. Outside the sun sidled toward the horizon. Ryan rubbed damp palms against his jeans. He'd officially put this off long enough to be considered a coward. Sure, he could use the boisterous family as an excuse, but that's what it would be.

He stood and held his hand out to Piper. "I hate to interrupt this, but I need to steal her away for a little while."

The old man had started snoring twenty minutes ago. Before that Manuel had taken to his room and toys. The lovers smiled at one another.

"I'll make sure he knocks," Gabriella said.

"Ah, it's the little one I'm worried about." Ryan laughed.

"Oh, Madre Maria, help me," she said, burying her face in Matthew's shoulder.

Ryan tugged Piper from her seat and toward the screened door.

She gave a small wave before turning to follow. Her raised hand moved to a lock of her loose copper strands, twirling it as she walked beside him. With a small tug he angled her away from the bunkhouse and into the vines.

"Walk with me?" As they ambled down the green-cordoned path, his nerves quivered.

"I'm liable to lapse into a food coma, if I sit again. But...I could be okay with a sex coma. At least I'd get some physical activity." The seductress wound her hair and bit her bottom lip as she gave him a sidelong glance.

"I almost blew you up, Piper."

Her steps faltered. Dust wafted from gritty earth. Afraid of what he'd see in her eyes, Ryan continued walking.

"But you didn't." Her sweet voice crossed the distance between them.

His steps ground to a halt, but he continued to stare at the infinite rows of green. "I knew about the shipment and had decided to leave them. It wasn't my mission," he scoffed. "I didn't want to step foot inside the prison because I was a guilty coward. Didn't want to see the future I'd doomed them to. Alma. Alisa. I only saved them because of you."

The truth tasted bitter on his tongue.

"That's not true. You wouldn't do anything you didn't believe to be right. No matter the orders."

"I'd like to think so, but I've done so many bad things in the name of good."

Her head nuzzled between his shoulder blades and her long, surprisingly strong, arms hugged his middle. "Your good outweighs the bad. The needs of the many outweigh that of the few. It doesn't make the decisions any easier. Most people don't have the courage to make those difficult judgments. And the hardest part is living with them."

Through his shirt she kissed him, and then stretched onto tiptoes. Her soft lips brushed his nape. "You are good. Honest. Brave. Caring. Selfless. Loyal."

"Because of you. For you." Ryan turned toward Piper and held her face. Every question found its answer in her eyes. He smothered her face in kisses. "I'll be right back." He stepped around her with a big, stupid grin on his face.

"Oh, hell no." Her hands shot to her hips. She tried for pissed, but couldn't quite hide the smirk. "I'm done with this cloak and dagger business. What is it? Where are you going?"

"Seriously, you didn't like it? The adrenaline? Sense of accomplishment at the end of the mission?"

"Sure, scared out of my mind. Heart beating out of my chest." Her voice laced with sarcasm. Her forceful huff billowed a few strands around her hair, and then she shrugged. "Aside from the fear of you getting shot again and the killing part, I love it."

"I love you," he blurted.

Her mouth gaped. She brought her hand up to cover it, but stopped. She pointed. "*I* said, I love it. What did you say?"

Ryan ran at her and caught her below her perfect ass. He hoisted her up high on his chest. Her legs cinched around his torso. Locking on her bronze eyes, he spoke slowly. "I love you, Piper Vega. I don't want to live a day without you."

Her teeth gleamed in the final rays of sunset. "I knew it. Well, hoped it really."

He kissed between her breasts, turned, and headed for the bunkhouse.

"Sex coma was a good idea, huh?" she asked, her fingers sliding gently through his hair.

"Perfect, but first I have to make two calls. One to tell my mother I'm moving to Los Angeles. The other to my commander to make certain Izar is eliminated, tell him I'm transferring to the L.A. office, and see about getting you a job. If you want it?"

"You think I'm cut out for this line of work?"

"Hell yes. I'm not keen on you dodging bullets, but you're a natural problem solver, quick on your feet, and ballsy." He set her down inside the door and snagged the phone. "You have ten minutes to get naked, sweet. If I go missing, one of the two of them has snatched me through the phone."

She stretched up and pulled his lower lip through her teeth. "I'd travel through hell to find you, Ryan."

"I know you would."

With one hand, she shoved him back. "I'll be waiting." She smiled and closed the door in his face.

He chuckled and hit redial, putting off the call to his mother as long as he could. Old habits and all. After beeps and his call sign and more beeps, Rhonda answered. "Voice confirmation complete. Agent Noble," she sniffled, "how may I direct your call?"

"Commander Tucker, please. Are you okay?"

"Commander Tucker...is dead, sir."

WARRIOR MINE
A BASE BRANCH NOVEL

A silver fox learns new tricks.

The Base Branch office in Washington D.C. is so heavily fortified it makes Fort Knox look like a 7-Eleven. After twenty years in covert ops, nothing fazes Commander Vail Tucker. When a lightning bolt of feminine fury crashes into the interrogation room, holds him at gunpoint, and takes over the task with his prisoner, he's more than surprised. She escapes without a trace, but Vail is unable to remain dispassionate. He must know what is so important the beguiling woman would risk her life to find it.

Carmen Ruez is deadly and desperate—a combustible combination. Born into the remnants of the Arellano Felix Organization, drugs and violence kept her in a gilded cage—until a twist of fate showed her the roots of their riches, making her yearn for freedom. She works for it. Fights for it. But her brother crosses the line to keep her loyal to the treacherous family she is determined to leave behind.

Following instinct, Vail uncovers Carmen's motives and is galvanized by a protective instinct he hadn't known he possessed. Determination and desire force them to work together to defeat those loyal to Carlos Ruez and the AFO. But are those traits enough to make them fight for a future together?

DANGER MINE
A BASE BRANCH NOVEL

One determined to avoid it. One determined to conquer it. Both on a wayward mission and unable to deny it.

Khani Slaughter has dealt with danger from the day of her conception. Thirty one years dealing with the bullshit and she knows how to attack it, defeat it, and avoid it. Yet, for some unfathomable reason, she gravitates toward it. When you're the head and sometimes deadly hands of the Base Branch, the special operations force for the United Nations, hazard pervades. Her personal life, though, is restricted territory for trouble. No strings flings. That's what she went for. Uncomplicated rolls in the sack. That was all she allowed. Or it had been until, the rookie showed up.

Base Branch operative, King Street takes danger and molds it to his benefit. Only, there's not much advantage in screwing the boss when regret sends her across an ocean. The desire to make her see him for more than the a mistake on her and humanity's part places his wide frame directly in her path.

He is cocky and way too brash. Not at all what she wants. But when her brother goes missing he is who she needs. Someone willing to navigate a wasteland, dodge bullets and her prickly demeanor to help rescue her only family. Just maybe, in the process they can save each other from their painful pasts.

Megan Mitcham was born and raised among the live oaks and shrimp boats of the Mississippi Gulf Coast, where her enormous family still calls home. She attended college at the University of Southern Mississippi where she received a bachelor's degree in curriculum, instruction, and special education. For several years Megan worked as a teacher in Mississippi. She married and moved to South Carolina and began working for an international non-profit organization as an instructor and co-director.

In 2009 Megan fell in love with books. Until then, books had been a source for research or the topic of tests. But one day she read *Mercy* by Julie Garwood. And oh, Mercy, she was hooked!

Megan lives in Southern Arkansas where she pens heart pounding romantic thriller novels and window-steaming erotic romance. For information on releases and giveaways subscribe at meganmitcham.com!

Facebook: @MeganMMMitcham
Twitter: MeganMitchamAuthor
Pinterest: MeganMitcham5
Goodreads: Megan_Mitcham
Website: www.meganmitcham.com

FOR INFORMATION ON NEW RELEASES & GIVEAWAYS, SIGN UP FOR MEGAN'S NEWSLETTER AT WWW.MEGANMITCHAM.COM.